TWISTED JUSTICE

M. A. COMLEY

This book is dedicated to the one person who has stood by me through thick and thin throughout my life, my beautiful Mother, Jean.

Thank you to the wonderful support of all The Book Club members and to those who allowed me to use their names in this book.

Special thanks as always go to my talented editor Stefanie Spangler Buswell and to Karri Klawiter for her cover design expertise.

My heartfelt thanks go to my wonderful proofreaders Joseph and Tara, for spotting all the lingering nits.

New York Times and USA Today bestselling author M A
Comley
Published by Jeamel Publishing limited
Copyright © 2015 M A Comley
Digital Edition, License Notes

OTHER BOOKS BY
M A COMLEY
Blind Justice
Cruel Justice
Impeding Justice
Final Justice
Foul Justice
Guaranteed Justice
Ultimate Justice
Virtual Justice
Hostile Justice
Tortured Justice
Rough Justice
Dubious Justice
Calculated Justice
Twisted Justice
Forever Watching You (DI Miranda Carr thriller)
Wrong Place (DI Sally Parker thriller)
No Hiding Place (DI Sally Parker thriller)
Web of Deceit (DI Sally Parker Novella with Tara Lyons) due
Jan 2016
Evil In Disguise – a novel based on True events
Deadly Act (Hero series novella)
Torn Apart (Hero Series #1)
End Result (Hero Series #2)
Sole Intention (Intention Series #1)
Grave Intention (Intention Series #2)
Merry Widow (A Lorne Simpkins short story)
It's A Dog's Life (A Lorne Simpkins short story)
A Time To Heal (A Sweet Romance)
A Time For Change (A Sweet Romance)
High Spirits
The Temptation Series (Romantic Suspense/New Adult
Novellas)
Past Temptation (available now)
Lost Temptation (available now)
Keep in touch with the author at
http://www.facebook.com/pages/Mel-Comley/264745836884860
http://melcomley.blogspot.com
Subscribe to newsletter

ISBN-13:978-1522753865

ISBN-10:1522753869

TWISTED JUSTICE

PROLOGUE

Ferocious fire raging beneath her surface, Claire Knight cast a distinctive look over her family, who stood nervously before her. They awaited her instructions with fear and trepidation etched on their faces. She ruled over them like a general commanding a squad of able and willing soldiers. Sometimes, however, her family needed gentle persuasion to remind them that she really did know best.

Claire Knight was the type of woman who, when rattled, could put an erupting Mount Vesuvius to shame. She scanned the worried faces of her three beautiful offspring. Mostly, she felt pride for the women, even if they weren't as smart as she was at times. Inwardly, she accepted their tiny flaws, aware they would need to be exceptional to match her abilities in this life, but outwardly, she had no trouble displaying how much her children annoyed her when they had the audacity to bombard her with dumb questions after the years she'd spent moulding them into near replicas of herself.

"And Lucy is all right with this, Mum?" Olga asked, swiping at her twitching nose after the drugs she'd just snorted.

Olga was referring to the only daughter absent from the meeting. Claire had felt it best not to involve her at this stage, if at all, in the plan, after the fresh round of doubts Lucy had issued only last week concerning certain aspects of her mother's full-on life.

"Of course she is," Claire lied, flashing a smile. "It's time you were setting off. Take the old car, not the new one. Leave it in the car park and grab a taxi if you're at all worried, or if someone sees you arriving back to shore." Teagan and Helen frowned at each other.

"Don't bloody start having doubts now. It's too late for that," she shouted, making them jump.

"No doubts, Mother, just a little apprehensive about what Lucy will say when she finds out." Teagan swept her curly, chestnut-coloured hair over her right shoulder.

Teagan was the one who most resembled Claire, in looks and spirit. The pair had shared more arguments over the years than the rest of the family put together. "Follow the instructions to the letter—that's all you have to do—and leave Lucy to me. She'll know this is for the best, come the end. What's with the look, Teagan? Don't you trust me on this?"

Teagan sighed heavily. "Yes, Mum. You know best. I'm sorry to question you," she replied, repeating the same dictum she'd been forced to say since she was six years old, since her life of crime had commenced under her mother's demonstrative leadership.

Throughout their childhood, all the kids had been desperate to feel their mother's love, so much so that they had been willing to regularly break the law and to even, when necessary, kill for Claire Knight...

CHAPTER ONE

Teagan and Helen set off towards the marina at Leigh-on-Sea. The slow-moving traffic agitated Teagan as she drove the two-hour journey accompanied by a selection of number-one hits from 2015 on the CD she'd purchased at the weekend.

With the marina just ahead of them, Teagan turned down the car stereo and looked at her sister. "Are you okay? You look green around the gills already, and we ain't even aboard the boat yet, sis."

Helen pulled in a long breath and let it escape slowly through her lips. "Would you hate me if I said I wanted to back out?"

"Nope. I feel the same way. However, if we don't do this, we'll feel the wrath of our dear mother."

"Yeah, we're buggered either way. If we get caught, we'll spend years behind bars, and if we don't go through with it, the old dear will probably ostracise us."

Teagan laughed. "I can't see her doing that, hon. We're too damn valuable to her, but I get your drift. If we follow Mum's instructions to the letter, there's no reason why we should get caught."

"Yeah, okay. It's what happens afterwards that's bugging me. I'm not sure I'll ever be able to face Lucy again after we carry out the deed. Why does it have to be Ryan we go after?"

Teagan shrugged. "At the end of the day, sis, we're just doing as we're told, like the soldiers of war she's instilled into us. Maybe one day we'll find a way of getting out from under her spell. Have you managed to squirrel away any money yet?"

"Nope, every time I manage to store away some cash, a major bill crops up."

"Ah, the beauty of living in the capital, eh?" Teagan parked the car at the back of the gravelled car park. She slapped her sister's bare thigh peeking out beneath her denim miniskirt. "It's show-time, sis. Time to flaunt our goods."

"Okay, just give me a couple of minutes to prepare myself."

"Not going to happen, sweet cheeks. You've had the two-hour trip over here to prepare yourself. Let's get this over with before we both get cold feet."

The two women got out of the car. Teagan tucked her arm through her sister's and felt the vibrations of her trembling body. "Hey, we're gonna be fine. You worry too much."

Helen shook her head. "I don't worry enough, you mean. If I worried too much, I wouldn't be in this shit now, and I would've left the restraints of our mother effing years ago."

"Stop whining. We're here now, and there's no turning back. Now, where's that award-winning smile of yours?" Helen turned to face her, fluttered her eyelashes, and smiled broadly. "Er... would you mind toning that down a bit? Make it more welcoming, perhaps?"

Helen exhaled another weary breath. "I was joking, Tea. Where's your bloody sense of humour gone?"

"Sorry. I'm just as wound up about this as you are. Come on, let's knock him dead. We have a big fish to reel in."

The pair supported each other as they tottered on their four-inch stilettos towards the dock where they'd arranged to meet their brother-in-law. Teagan hitched up her miniskirt even higher as she approached the boat, and Ryan held out a hand to help her aboard. A wolf whistle sounded from the boat tied up alongside. Seething inside, Teagan threw the lecherous sailor a 'you couldn't afford this bag of shit' kind of look. Her choice of clothing for the day was supposed to attract only one man's attention. Her mother would be furious if she knew Helen and Teagan were attracting a crowd of onlookers.

"You both look stunning... umm... the thing is, ladies, I'm going to have to ask you to remove your shoes."

Teagan tickled her brother-in-law under the chin. "And I don't want to hear about your foot fetish, sweets, if that's okay with you. You can practise that kind of thing on Lucy when you get home."

Ryan tutted. "Ever the joker, aren't you, Tea? It's for safety reasons, I can assure you. Want me to fetch a pair of Lucy's deck shoes for both of you?"

Both women cringed and screwed up their noses in unison.

He laughed. "I get the hint. She's new anyway, so there really shouldn't be any splinters anywhere. Just be extra careful."

"This is *stunning*, Ryan. It must have set you back a packet?" Teagan asked, her gaze admiring the glistening wood under the warming sun's rays.

"Let's just say I had to be a tad economical with the truth when Lucy asked how much I paid for the boat."

"Go on, let us in on the secret?" She made the sign of the cross on her chest. "Promise not to tell Lucy."

He shook his head, and a smile stretched his full lips, revealing his pearly whites. "If you plucked the figure of forty grand out of the air, you'd not be far off the mark."

Teagan's eyes widened. "What? You're teasing me, right? Lucy wouldn't allow you to spend that much on a crummy boat. Umm… granted this is a super-nice crummy boat."

"Let's just say that the transaction occurred after some very nifty personal accounting on my part."

"You were always good at that, according to Mum," Helen grumbled just loud enough for him to hear.

He roared with laughter. "Call it perks of the trade."

"Yeah, I've never met an honest solicitor yet." Teagan laughed riotously.

Ryan's eyebrows raised alternatively—a little party trick of his that apparently only he found amusing—as his eyes swept over Teagan's heaving breasts. She played up to him and thrust her boobs out farther. Helen jabbed her in the back and groaned disapprovingly under her breath.

Teagan's shoulders slumped again, and she took a few steps towards Ryan. "What are we waiting for? You said you'd show us how fast this baby can go."

"Love it when I'm dealing with eager ladies." He chortled. "Who's up for helping me out?"

"What do you need us to do? I have to warn you, I've never been good on boats." Helen swallowed noisily.

"Why don't I give you a guided tour first, and then we'll cast off. I should make you aware where everything is, just in case we run into any trouble."

Helen's hand flew up to her chest, and she gasped. "Trouble? What kind of bloody trouble? Did you hear me when I said I'm not good on boats?"

"As my old scoutmaster used to say: 'It's always better to be prepared.' In my book, his advice has always been invaluable."

"Right you are, then. Where first?" Teagan asked, shooting her sister a warning glance.

Ryan turned his back and led the way through to the cabin.

"What did I do?" Helen mouthed innocently at her sister.

"Behave yourself. Go with the flow and don't raise his suspicions."

Helen huffed out a breath and mumbled, "Whatever." Then she followed Ryan into the cabin.

He pushed open a cabin that was laid out as a seating area. "This converts into a double bed and is where all the action takes place once we're out at sea, tied up, bobbing around on the waves." He leaned in and said conspiratorially, "Not a word to the boat builders. This particular Viking is supposed to be for the inland waterways only, but I just had to bring her down here to show her off to you girls."

The thought of bedding the man, if that was what he was implying, caused bile to emerge in Teagan's throat. On more than one occasion over the past few years, she'd pictured Lucy and him getting it on, and the repulsive pictures danced around her mind again. Ryan wasn't exactly ugly—in fact the total opposite was true—but he had never really appealed to her sexually. Other men could eat her up with their eyes, and she would fall into bed with them after a few drinks, but Ryan creeped her out for some reason. What Lucy found attractive in this man bewildered her at times. *Each to their own, I suppose!* Some people liked the tanned blond, Paul Newman kind of look. She happened to be one of those who *didn't*.

She preferred her men burly and scarred up as if they'd truly lived life to the full and not been afraid to get stuck in when the going got tough—like her ex, Frank. Deep down, she regretted the way their relationship had ended. She shook her head, dislodging the vile image of Frank's demise. "Where do you drive the thing, Ryan? I'm not interested in where you sleep or do *other* things."

"I *pilot* the damn thing upstairs. Come on, I can see how impatient you are to get going, Teagan. Not so sure about Helen, though. Maybe you should stay behind on the dock if you feel that queasy, babe?"

Helen waved a hand at him. "I'll be fine. Just make sure you point out where the rubber dinghy is in case I need to make a quick getaway."

Ryan squeezed past the girls, ensuring his crotch brushed back and forth a few times against their thighs in the confined space. Teagan suppressed a laugh at her sister's horrified face. She thought Helen was going to projectile vomit over Ryan there and then.

Once he was out of earshot, Helen whispered, "Gross, he thinks he's bloody David Beckham."

"Just smile. Don't let him see that he's getting to you. Did you spy all the food and champers he's bought? I have a feeling he believes we're here to indulge in more than taking a tour around his new acquisition."

Helen shuddered. "Eww… I feel even sicker now than when I arrived."

"Come on, let's catch him up. The sooner we get out of here, the better."

They stepped back on the deck and found Ryan waiting for them. He motioned to the three steps leading up to the cockpit. The cramped area contained a bench seat at the back with a single helm seat for the pilot. "Cosy, eh?" Ryan asked, shoulders pulled back, beaming with pride for his new acquisition.

"*Cramped*, I'd call it, but then we're used to the luxury of living in mansions. I have to say forty grand seems a bit excessive, or did you exaggerate that sum?" Teagan winked at him, aware that all men tended to embellish the truth about their expenditure when trying to impress the opposite sex.

Ryan's smile slipped. Teagan's remark had obviously offended her brother-in-law.

"It's always good to work up to managing one of the big boys. I'll get used to this one over the coming months then trade her in when more funds become available. Our place has taken over two hundred grand to renovate. We have to draw the line somewhere. This will do for now."

"Good, Lucy deserves the best after the year she's had."

"Yep, losing the baby at ten weeks was hard on both of us. That will be rectified soon enough, if you know what I mean?" He chuckled at his own inane joke.

Teagan clapped her hands together. "Enough chatting. How about you show us what this baby can do out in the open sea?"

"Well, I'm warning you, I'm not going to push her. She's new, and you need to take care of the engine for the first few months or so. Plus, like I said earlier, she's not really a sea-faring vessel."

Helen tutted. "Then why the hell did you buy her?"

Teagan shot her sister another warning glance. "Now, now, sis, there's no need for you to get touchy about this. We know you're not really looking forward to the trip."

"If you're gonna gripe about things all the time, Helen, maybe it would be better if you and your foul mood remained here, while I show Teagan a good time out at sea."

Teagan cringed again. "She'll be fine. It's trepidation that's making her tetchy. Isn't it, hon?"

"I'll just sit here and be quiet. How's that?" Helen threw herself onto the leather-clad bench, folded her arms, and mimicked a pouting teenager.

"Ignore her. What do you want me to do, Ryan?" Teagan asked.

"We need to cast off. I'll help untie the boat from the dock. If you hold on to the final rope, I'll climb aboard again, start up the engine, and you can hop back on. How's that?" Ryan replied, his smile returning.

"Great, in this bloody *skirt*? What if I fall in?"

"You won't. The boat won't move off until I put it into drive."

Reluctantly, Teagan scooted down the steps and towards the stern of the boat, regretting that she hadn't chosen to wear nautical clothing of jeans, a T-shirt and trainers. "I won't slip in my bare feet, will I?"

"Nah, you'll be fine. The deck isn't slippery in the afternoon, only in the mornings at this time of year."

"Maybe it would be better to take us out in the springtime instead," Teagan announced uneasily.

"Are you telling me that you're scared now, too?" Ryan tilted his head.

"I didn't say that. Bugger, okay, just ignore me." Teagan hopped back onto the dock and adjusted her skirt, which had ridden farther up her thighs.

Ryan landed close on the dock beside her and groaned gutturally. "No need to adjust anything on my account."

Teagan thumped his arm. "Cheeky sod. I have a new dilemma for you."

"Which is?"

She held out her beautifully manicured hands, red at the pointed tips. "What about my nails?"

"Are they false?"

"Yep, and they cost a packet, too. I'd hate to break any."

"Bloody hell! You women are impossible at times. All right, leave the untying to me. You just hold the rope when I'm done. How's that?"

Teagan fluttered her eyelashes several times and smiled a toothy smile. *Men are so easy to wrap around your finger when you're dressed like a tart. Maybe it was wise wearing this getup after all.* "You're an angel," she told him sweetly.

Once all the ropes were untied, Ryan handed one chunky length of rope to Teagan and jumped back aboard the boat. He shouted over his shoulder, "Wait until I start the engine. I'll tell you when to jump back on the boat, okay?"

"Aye, aye, Captain." Teagan could feel the nerves begin to jangle in her tummy at the thought of slipping and falling into the bitterly cold water between the boat and the dock. She pushed the image firmly out of her mind when she heard the diesel engine roar into life.

"Now, Teagan!" Ryan shouted above the engine noise.

Teagan threw the rope onto the wooden deck and quickly climbed aboard the vessel. She huffed out a relieved breath when she completed the manoeuvre without any mishaps. Super pleased with her efforts, she re-joined Helen and Ryan at the helm. "Yay, I'm a fully-fledged ship hand, or whatever the correct title is," she cried elatedly, to her sister's obvious disgust.

The boat eased away from the dock. Ryan guided it effortlessly past the nearby boats, up the narrow channel, and out towards the sea. "You did well, Teagan. Want to play hostess with the mostess once we get out in the open?"

"I'd love to. I noticed the spread down in the kitchen."

He laughed. "You mean the 'galley,' old girl."

Helen, looking greener by the second, clutched her sister's forearm and squeezed it. "Really, do you have to talk about food right now?"

"It'll wear off soon enough. Either that, or it will get ten times worse when we hit the open sea," Ryan teased cruelly.

Teagan uncurled her sister's fingers a little, easing the excruciating pain in her forearm. "He's joking. Take no notice."

"I wish he wouldn't. I think it would be better if I had a bucket close by." Helen ran her thumb between her breasts. "I can feel it here."

"Ryan, is there a bucket around?" Teagan called out.

Without taking his eyes off the course ahead of him, he replied, "There's one in the cupboard in the galley. It's got the mop in it."

"Gross. That's gonna stink," Helen complained.

"What's the alternative? Do it here and mess up Ryan's beautiful new boat?"

"All right, don't go on at me. I can't help it if I feel sick."

Teagan widened her eyes, letting her sister know in no uncertain terms how annoying she was being. Then she went in search of the bucket. After swilling it out a few times with soapy water, trying to get rid of the stench, she returned.

As the vessel continued along the Thames and out to sea, Helen retched a couple of times, but nothing untoward surfaced. Teagan took the opportunity to sit and enjoy the view, even though she shivered now and then because of the chilly December air. Again, she cursed her choice of garments. She glanced down at her breasts and saw that her nipples were extended, letting everyone know how cold she was.

"Everything all right, ladies? Enjoying the ride, are you?" Ryan shouted.

"We're bearing up back here. How long before we reach the sea?" Teagan thought she spotted the harbour walls up ahead but wasn't quite sure if her eyes were playing tricks on her.

"Another couple of minutes, then we'll have freedom to see what this baby can do, within reason of course."

Teagan leaned towards Helen. "How are you holding up?"

"So far I'm managing to keep my breakfast down. Not sure what I'll be like when I lay eyes on that food, though. Do we have to go through that?"

Teagan nodded. "We need to get him a little tipsy. Just leave it to me. Where's your bag?"

Helen pointed down at the handbag she'd shoved behind her calves. "It's safe. I didn't want to risk it flying overboard if we hit a stray wave or a seagull swept down and plucked it up."

"You're impossible. As if either of those things is going to happen? Just be prepared. You've got the weapon, right?"

Helen nodded. "Yep, don't worry. It's all in hand."

Still whispering and hopeful that the boat's engine would prevent Ryan from overhearing their conversation, Teagan said, "Let's make him nice and comfortable before we start discussing business. Follow my lead on that, okay?"

"Suits me. Just don't friggin' offer me any of that greasy food he's taken the trouble of supplying." She gagged and moved the bucket under her chin.

Teagan rubbed her hand up and down her sister's back. "Don't think about it. Take a few gulps of air, and it'll pass, I promise."

"At last!" Ryan shouted. "Here we go, ladies. Brace yourselves. Looks like it's going to be a tad choppy out at sea."

"Oh fuck! Why me? Why did I agree to bloody come out here?" Helen complained as the choppy waves bashed the bottom of the boat, making Teagan and Helen's bodies jolt and bob rhythmically.

Teagan wedged the bucket between her sister's knees. The motion of the boat was affecting her cast-iron stomach, making her wonder which of them would end up vomiting first. She took her own advice and sucked in a lungful of fresh air.

"Do we have to go far?" Helen pleaded, her face paler than the finest white sand found in the Sahara desert.

"Come on, just enjoy the ride. Let the freedom of the experience wash over you. Allow the exhilaration to blow away the cobwebs as you feel the wind beneath your wings."

"Shut the fuck up, Ryan. You're talking crap, as usual," Teagan shot back at him as her own discomfort multiplied beyond recognition. "How far before we can drop anchor?"

"You're not winding me up, are you? Do you really feel crap, the pair of you?"

"Yeah, we're both feeling super crap now."

"I'll turn back, then. It makes no odds to me. We can have lunch in dry dock."

Panic struck and urged Teagan to reject the plan. "No! Don't do that. We'll be fine for a few more minutes. Won't we, Helen?" She looked over her shoulder at the marina, which was getting smaller with each bounce of a wave beneath the boat. *Yes, a few more minutes will suffice.*

"Let's just go round the coast a little, and then I'll drop anchor. How does that sound to you?" Ryan pointed at the coastline jutting out ahead of them.

"That's fine," Teagan shouted. She glanced at her sister. "Almost there now. Are you ready for this?"

"Yep, even more so now after what he's just bloody put me through."

Several minutes later, Ryan tinkered with the controls and the boat slowed to a halt. He leapt out of his chair and sprinted to the stern to drop the anchor overboard. At about the same time, Teagan's heart rate escalated when she realised the time had come to start playing up to Ryan. The notion didn't sit well with her. Nevertheless, it was essential to their plan.

CHAPTER TWO

"Do you two want to sit up here and eat your food or join me downstairs in the galley?"

The twinkle in his eye made her want to retch. "I think it would be better up here where there's more room and fresh air."

"Right you are. I'll be back shortly. Be good." Ryan winked and ran down the steps.

"Damn, I don't have my shoes," Helen said.

"I'm not with you. Why do you want them?"

"I was going to whack him in the head with the heel if he causes any trouble."

Teagan winced. "Okay, then that could be a problem. Maybe we should go downstairs in that case, to the kitchen. I noticed some butcher's knives hanging up on the wall."

Helen snorted. "What are you going to do? Just take one down in plain sight?"

"Hardly, Helen. Grant me with some sense. You could distract him long enough for me to grab one," Teagan pointed out.

"And shove it where?"

Teagan looked down at the skimpy outfit she was wearing then at her tiny clutch bag lying on the floor. She threw her arms out to the side. "Crap! I don't know. I'm sure open to suggestions!"

Helen shrugged. "You're supposed to be the one with all the brains. You got us into this mess. It's up to you to get us out of it."

"Jeez, thanks for the bloody support. Shh… he's coming back."

Ryan appeared, holding a tray of pastry-filled canapés fresh out of their Marks and Spencer packets and placed them alongside Helen on the leather bench. "I'll just go down and grab the champagne. Be right back, ladies."

Teagan blocked his path and smiled. "You've done enough, sweetie. I'll get the drinks. You enjoy the chow."

He winked. "Well, I won't argue with you. Just bring the bottle and the glasses. I'll open it for you."

Teagan swiftly trotted down the steps and into the galley. She eyed the knives. A medium-sized blade situated halfway along the rack drew her attention. She tucked it down the back of the waistband of her miniskirt, settling the knife against her spine. The cold blade against her bare skin made her gasp. Her hand flew up to her mouth. She hoped neither Ryan nor Helen had heard. Neither of them appeared or called out, so she let out a relieved sigh. Before she returned to the cockpit, she searched around for something else she and Helen could use as a weapon. On the small table she saw two condiment pots. "That'll do." She grabbed the pot of pepper and added it to the tray, along with the three glasses and the bottle. Then she headed back to join the others.

"We thought you'd got lost. Here, let me take that," Ryan said, relieving her of the tray and setting it down next to the food. He picked up the bottle and, without much effort, popped the cork. He filled the three glasses, careful that the effervescent liquid didn't exceed the halfway mark. He handed a glass to Helen and then one to Teagan. Holding his glass in front of him, he proposed a toast. "To us! May the family go from strength to strength under your mother's remarkable leadership. What a gal she is. One I wouldn't like to get on the wrong side of, that's for sure," he added with a chuckle.

Helen and Teagan sipped their drinks and stared at each other without saying a word.

"Tuck in, girls. I don't want to hear any nonsense about you being on a diet, either." His eyes ran the length of their stunning figures before he continued, "You both look super fit to me. Must be the fantastic genes you've inherited from your mother, eh? She's a pretty fit bird for her age, too."

Teagan flashed her teeth at him even though she was seething inside about the way he was referring to her mother. "Do you want to discuss business now, Ryan?"

"Can't we have our eats first?" he asked, shoving a whole salmon-filled vol-au-vent into his mouth.

"I think Helen and I both still feel a little queasy. You carry on, though."

"Thanks. I'm starving. You girls seem really tense. You need to loosen up a little. Do you want me to put a CD on to really get this party started?"

"Let's leave that for now. We're really only here to discuss business. Maybe when we've dealt with that, we can have a quick boogie before heading back to shore. How's that?"

"Sure. Whatever you say. What's this all about anyway? Over the phone, your mother mentioned something concerning the paperwork I was looking into." He shuffled his feet.

"That's right. Specifically the deeds," Teagan replied, wary about his reaction. He was coming across shifty to her. He knew full well why they were there and what they intended to discuss. The question was: why was he toying with them?

He downed the remains of his glass and refilled it before he spoke again. "Here's the crunch—the deeds, or more to the point, what your mother was hoping to do regarding the deeds, is a no-go."

Teagan's eyes narrowed. "No-go? In what respect? Mum's paid you damn good money to ensure everything would go through without a hitch. Are you telling us you've screwed up or gone back on your promise?"

"In a way, yes. Listen, Teagan, the thing is, my business is on the up. I'm becoming well-known and respected in my field, and I don't really want to do anything to jeopardise that."

Teagan placed her glass on the tray and twisted to stand in front of him, inches from his nose. She prodded him in the chest. "You've got a bloody short memory, Ryan. If it wasn't for our mum setting you up in business in the first place, you'd still be skivvying for your old firm on minimum frigging wage."

Ryan took a step back. "Hardly, love. I was never on minimum wage at Donaldson's. Hey, and I don't appreciate hearing you shoving it down my throat how much I owe your mum either. She knows how grateful I am for giving me the chance to set up on my own."

"Then *prove* it. Hand over the deeds to those properties, *now*," Teagan ordered, a touch of underlying threat in her tone.

"It's not going to happen, Teagan. I've thought long and hard about this. Lucy will tell you how many sleepless nights I've had churning this over. However, she has no idea about the untenable position your mother has put me in. My decision is final. I will *not* let your mother, or you, bully me into doing things that don't sit comfortably with me any longer. I've come to realise that the risks far outweigh the gains, and when that occurs, it's time for me to take a step back. I know your mum is going to hate me for this. But she's just going to have to find some other mug to tamper with those deeds."

Teagan's eyes widened momentarily but narrowed as her mind raced. Instead, she smiled sweetly at Ryan. "You know what? I really admire you having the balls to stand up to Mum like this,

Ryan. I've wanted to do it for years. Haven't you, Helen?" She turned to face Helen and winked at her.

Her sister nodded but kept her mouth shut. She knew when to keep schtum and let Teagan do all the talking.

When her gaze returned to Ryan, Teagan could see his features had slackened with relief.

"Phew! You don't know how good it is to hear you say that, Teagan. I had a feeling you were getting fed up with your mother's tyrannical ways."

Teagan's head dipped to her chest. "You're right, Ryan. A person can only take so much. Mum's got to understand that none of us are getting any younger and the time has come to settle down and enjoy life without having to look over our shoulders, waiting for the coppers to arrive on our doorstep. I'm with you on that score, one thousand percent, matey." She slapped him on the shoulder. "I'll just take the deeds back to Mum and tell her to shove it, eh? Tell her this is the final time you're willing to help out. How's that?"

He smiled. "Well, perhaps put it slightly more tactfully than that. If you're sure she'll accept that, I've got them downstairs in my bag. I'll be right back."

"She will. Times are changing for all of us. She'll accept you wanting to move on to bigger and better things, Ryan, providing you don't go back on your word this time, of course."

Once Ryan was out of earshot, Teagan rushed to Helen's side. "Hopefully that bullshit will persuade him to do the right thing, but just in case, we need to be ready to make our move. As soon as he returns, I want you to trip him up. I'll take it from there, okay?"

Helen sighed. "I'm still feeling a little under the weather, Tea. I'm not sure I can go through with this."

"Which is why I told you not to get involved any more than tripping him up. Give me a break; *I'll* be doing all the dirty work, not you." Teagan could tell her sister was feeling better and was pulling a fast one, because her cheeks were looking rosier than they had when the boat trip began.

"All right," Helen replied reluctantly. "I just want to get this over with and back on dry land as soon as we can. Can we do that, Tea?"

Teagan ran a gentle hand down her sister's pretty cheek. "I'm sure we can have this all wrapped up in a few minutes, sweetie. Keep the faith, eh? Have I ever let you down yet?"

Helen rolled her eyes. "Not on that front, no!"

They heard Ryan below them and quickly separated. Teagan stood back against the side of the boat while Helen took a deep breath and prepared herself for her part in the arrangement.

Ryan appeared at the top of the steps and waved the deeds in front of him. He neglected to see Helen's outstretched leg and tumbled to the deck at Teagan's feet. "Oops, how clumsy of you, Helen."

The sisters chuckled as Teagan withdrew the knife from the back of her skirt and plunged it into Ryan's neck before he had a chance to get back on his feet.

The blood spurted, pooling rapidly around him. He tried to suppress the wound with his right hand, but the blood oozed quickly through his fingers. "What the fuck? Why, Teagan? Why?"

She answered him by stabbing the knife first in the other side of his neck then several times in his back. "Don't just sit there, Helen. Gather all the papers."

Helen appeared to be frozen to the bench, and the colour that had been seeping into her cheeks during their conversation moments earlier had swiftly vanished. She was staring down at her brother-in-law, open mouthed, as he gasped for air and wriggled on the deck like a fish out of water. However, his thrashing soon died down.

A lifetime seemed to pass before Ryan's body stilled at Teagan's feet. She placed two fingers on his neck to check for a pulse—and found none.

Teagan clicked her fingers in front of her sister's shocked face. "Okay, Helen, stay with me. Don't go melting down just yet. Have you got all the papers?"

Helen nodded, her eyes glued to Ryan's bloodied, motionless corpse.

"Right. We need to get out of here, sharp."

Helen shook her head vigorously. "How?"

"We'll have to take the dinghy. You organise that while I clear up here."

"'Clear up'? What do you mean?"

"All right, maybe that was the wrong term. I didn't intend to say 'clear up.' Maybe 'finish off' would be appropriate."

Helen cringed and ran a shaking hand over her face. "I don't want to know, do I?"

"No, sweetie, you don't. Just remember him as he used to be, all right?"

Helen rushed down the steps and left Teagan to finish off the task at hand. Stepping over Ryan's body, she removed the trays of food and drink from the bench and lifted the cushion. "There has to be one in here somewhere. He wouldn't be so daft not to have any aboard." She threw the ropes and life jackets aside, revealing the items she was looking for. Picking up the two flares, she punched the air with her fist. "There you are, you beauties." She leaned over the back of the bench to see Helen struggling to place the dinghy in the water at the stern. "Come on, tug it, Helen. You can do it, girl."

Helen turned in her direction. Trails of mascara marked either side of her face. "I can't. I'm too weak to lift it. You're going to have to help me, Tea."

For fuck's sake, woman! Can't you do anything frigging right? "I'll be with you in a tick. Let me prepare things up here first. Take a chill pill until then. Stop crying. We're nearly there."

"That's easy for you to say. I never wanted to get mixed up in this shit in the first place." Helen threw herself against the side of the boat, pouting as she crossed her arms.

Teagan decided to ignore her sister's childish behaviour and returned to the business at hand. She removed the cap from the two flares and got down on her knees, avoiding Ryan's pooling blood. She shoved one of the flares in his mouth, keeping the ignition end exposed. Then she went downstairs and into the galley, where she turned on the gas to the cooker and the oven before running back up the steps to Ryan's body. She picked up their handbags and dipped inside her own to find a lighter. Then she bent over and lit the end of the flare. It sparked into life immediately. She fled the area again, snatched up their shoes on the way, and threw the bags and the shoes into the dinghy. "Help me get it in the water. We don't have much time."

"What? What have you *done*? I thought we were just going to tug up the anchor and let the boat drift out here. Those were Mother's instructions."

"Shut the fuck up and get a move on. Now heave!"

Seconds later, they had lowered the dinghy into the water. They hopped aboard, and Teagan instructed Helen to start the motor, which again, she struggled with. "Jesus, do I have to do everything? Get out of the way." She pulled the starter cord, and the boat's engine *phut phutted* into life. Teagan picked up the flare and lit it, much to her sister's shock.

"No, Teagan. Don't do that, please—not to Ryan."

"What the fuck are you talking about? He's already dead. What does it matter what I do next?" She threw the erupting flare up onto the deck of the boat. Then she took control of the dinghy, directing it towards the shoreline at full pelt. "Keep your head down. She's going to blow any minute."

"Why? Why do this, Teagan? I don't know *you* anymore."

Teagan shrugged. "Someone's got to be ready to step up to the plate when Mum retires." The explosion drowned out her laughter. Blazing debris missed the dinghy by inches. In the height of the summer, the plan would have been impossible to execute. December was a different story entirely, since most people avoided the beach in the colder weather.

Teagan steered the boat towards Chalkwell Beach at Westcliffe-on-Sea, which was empty. Once the dinghy landed on the rocky shore, Teagan ordered, "Leg it, hon. Keep your shoes off and run as fast as you can."

"Ouch, the stones are killing my feet."

"Your frigging constant whinging is killing *me*. Do you want to get caught? You're going the right way about it."

They upped their pace as another small explosion struck Ryan's cruiser. "There's a taxi rank in the next road if I remember rightly."

"Then what? Pick up the car or return to Mum's?"

"Pick up the car, idiot. No need to get in Mum's bad books about ditching the car on top of everything else." A satisfied grin stretched across her lips. Teagan couldn't believe they'd pulled it off without being seen. *I guess not many folks venture down the beach in December.* She rubbed the goose bumps emerging on her arms and legs. Again, she cursed the clothes she was wearing. But it had all been worth it in the end.

The taxi driver was a little Chinese man who spoke relatively good English. "Where to, ladies?"

"The Marina at Leigh-on-Sea, please. Make it snappy," Teagan replied, watching the man raise a questioning eyebrow as he looked at them in his rear-view mirror. She answered him with a raised eyebrow of her own until he shrugged and started the car. She fidgeted with her handbag, and arranged it over the blood splattered across one side of her top, hoping the driver didn't spot it.

"I'm…" Helen started to speak. Teagan bashed her knee with her own, warning her not to say anything incriminating. Instead Helen folded her arms in annoyance.

When the driver dropped them off, Teagan paid the man without adding a tip, she was tight like that. They rushed back to their car and set off. Both of them expelled a lengthy breath, relieved that they hadn't been caught. All that was left for them to do now, was deal with the wrath of their mother upon their return.

CHAPTER THREE

Lorne burst into the kitchen, whistling the chorus from *I'm So Happy*. Everything was going so well in her life lately. It was good to be alive, surrounded by people she loved and admired.

"You're super chirpy this morning. Any reason?" Tony, her husband, held open his arms to welcome her.

"Just happy. For you, for me, for Charlie now that she has a regular boyfriend in tow."

"I figured Charlie's status was the main reason. It is fabulous to see her walking around here with a light heart and a certain spring in her step. I know I've told you thousands of times before, but at the risk of repeating myself, I'm going to tell you again anyway. That girl is an absolute credit to you, darling wife of mine."

"Hey, it's been a team effort, keeping her on the straight and narrow. I can't thank you enough for giving her the time to adjust, Tony."

He pecked the tip of her nose and squeezed her tightly. "Nonsense! We've all been forced to make adjustments over the past few years, what with me having to get used to this thing." He stretched out his prosthetic leg.

"Talking of which, have you had any pain lately?"

"A few niggles, but nothing a butch ex-MI6 agent can't handle."

Lorne laughed. "What's on your agenda today?"

He screwed up his nose. "Nothing much. The PI business is relatively quiet at the moment. Must be the time of year, what with Christmas approaching faster than a speeding bullet. I thought I'd give Charlie a hand today, cleaning out the kennels. I know she has an agility class to attend tonight with Sheba."

Lorne glanced over at the German shepherd sitting on her bed, looking at them with her head cocked. "She's a treasure, isn't she? Apparently, she was the top dog in her class last week. Not bad for a dog who someone heartlessly kicked out onto the street, eh?"

"Their loss is our gain. She's settled in well with us. Mind you, that's mainly down to Charlie's training and affection."

"Yep, she's a star. Right, I better grab a quick coffee and some toast and then set off for work."

"Ah, the hectic life of a detective inspector in the Metropolitan Police Force, which never fails to interfere with life's more pleasant moments."

Lorne's brow furrowed. "Why the sarcasm?"

Tony shrugged innocently. "No sarcasm intended. Purely stating facts. Maybe you're being a little oversensitive?"

She walked over to the toaster, popped two slices of multigrain bread in the slots, and switched on the kettle. "Is Charlie around?"

"Yep, she was up early; another one feeling chirpy this morning. She's out in the kennels, feeding the dogs."

"No matter how late she gets in the previous night, she never neglects her duties. Not sure how many youngsters can say they're capable of doing the same thing these days."

"She's twenty-one and no longer a teenager. That must count for something."

"You reckon? Will you remind me to ring Jade later this evening? She was talking about going to Italy with Luigi and the boys for Christmas. I'm reading that as a huge hint not to forget sorting out a convenient time to exchange presents before their trip."

Tony looked upset by the news. "Lucky for some. Maybe we could do that one year. Just book a flight and get away from it all."

"For a start, we don't have the money, and for another, you're forgetting I don't care much for flying."

"What about a cruise?" Tony asked.

"Seasick." The toast popped up, and Lorne spread it thickly with marmalade, no butter as she was cutting back on fats, then she poured her coffee in the Thermos cup sitting alongside the kettle. "I'm going to have this en route." She kissed Tony on the lips and ran out the back door. "Love you, Agent Boy," she called over her shoulder.

He appeared on the back step and wagged a finger at her. "I thought you promised never to call me that again."

She placed a finger to her lips. "Did I? Oops, it must have slipped my mind. See you later."

Shaking his head, Tony turned and walked back into the house as Lorne started the car and headed into London, before the rush-hour traffic had the chance to build up.

Her mood was still buoyant when she breezed into the incident room to find her partner, Katy, and Katy's fiancé, AJ, already at their desks. "Am I late?" she asked, looking up at the clock on the wall.

"No, I couldn't sleep, so AJ suggested we come in to work early."

Lorne cocked her head. "Really? Are you mad?"

AJ shrugged and pointed at Katy's bulging stomach. "When the little one can't sleep, he plays up. No point lying there getting wound up because neither of us can get some shut-eye."

"I can think of better things to do, AJ, than to begin your shift early." She winked at Katy, whose face had turned pink. "Ha, on second thoughts, if you'd kept it in your trousers in the first place, Katy would probably still be DI instead of me."

AJ's mouth dropped open, and Katy burst out laughing. "You tell him, Lorne. I'm fed up of saying it."

"Oh dear! I didn't realise it was a touchy subject. I was only teasing, I promise. Any new cases come in over the weekend?" Lorne added, swiftly changing the subject.

"Nothing as yet. It's still early. I'm tying up the paperwork for the child murder case from a few weeks ago, now the father is sitting in a remand cell."

"Three cheers on that one. Can't understand why people have kids if they're going to kill them at the first sign of trouble. That little boy didn't stand a chance with a thug like that for a father. Shame on the mother, too, for putting her son in harm's way. Okay, I'll get off my soap box now and see what awaits me in the office. Give me a shout if anything crops up."

Katy and AJ nodded and returned to their tasks. Lorne left them to it and marched into her office. She paused in the doorway and closed her eyes. The briefest whiff of Cool Water aftershave tickled her nostrils as she entered. She smiled endearingly. "Morning, Pete."

Of course, her deceased partner didn't answer. He rarely openly made contact with her, just left her clues now and again, letting her know he was around—like the KitKat wrapper she'd found in the back of the taxi when Baldwin's ex-partner had kidnapped her a few months before. A calmness descended in the wake of troubled waters when she recognised he was near. Her good friend and psychic, Carol, often told her that Pete was always around her, ensuring she was safe even when the odds were stacked firmly against her. That in itself was a source of great comfort to Lorne. She'd loved Pete as a brother and ribbed him constantly about his weight, but she'd loved him all the same.

Midway through tackling her post, Lorne heaved a sigh of relief when the phone interrupted her. She sat back in her chair and answered the call. "Hello, DI Warner. How can I help?"

"Are you busy?"

"Patti? Is that you?" Lorne sat upright when she recognised the local pathologist's voice.

"Who else would be calling you, standing out in the cold on a soggy December morning?"

Lorne glanced over at her office window, which was splattered with tiny rain droplets. "I hadn't noticed it was raining. Where are you?"

"Down at Leigh-on-Sea."

"Dare I ask what you're doing there?"

"Not really. But I think you should get your arse into gear and get over here ASAP!"

Lorne hitched her jacket off the back of the chair and placed one arm in the sleeve while she stood up. She recognised the seriousness of the situation if Patti was calling her directly from the scene. "I'm on my way. Give me your exact location."

"The marina. As quick as you can, Lorne. It's a biggie." Patti hung up.

Lorne raced into the incident room. "Katy, get your coat on."

A puzzled-looking Katy rushed over to the coat stand and slipped on her black woollen coat. "Dare I ask what this is about?"

"Your guess is as good as mine until we get there."

CHAPTER FOUR

The area was cordoned off with tape when Lorne and Katy arrived. Patti waved at them and motioned for them to join her.

"What's the mystery about, Patti?" Lorne enquired when the pathologist was close enough to hear.

"You'll find out soon enough. Come with me." Patti led them to the other end of the car park. A crane was nearby, with what appeared to be a burnt-out boat on the end of its wire.

"A boat?"

"Yes, but not just any old boat. This one had a dead body aboard," Patti said.

"Okay. Tell me you're not expecting us to get on that thing," Lorne said, anxiously surveying the charred vessel.

"You'd have a job. It's far too brittle for anyone to climb aboard to take a look around."

"But you've been on, yes?" Lorne asked.

Patti nodded. "Yes, I wanted to examine the body in situ but then realised the dangers and asked two of my men to take pictures of the scene before they transported the body off the vessel."

Lorne scanned the area for the sheeted remains. "So, where is it?"

"In the boathouse, at the insistence of a kind mechanic. Given the weather conditions, I was relieved to get it under cover. This way."

They made their way into a huge mechanic's workshop. Several men nodded hello when Lorne and Katy entered. The body was in a secluded area just inside the door, away from the mechanics' prying eyes.

Patti crouched and gently pulled back the sheet. Lorne gasped as Katy gagged.

Patti quickly covered the charred remains again. "Sorry, I should have warned you it wasn't pretty. Maybe, given your delicate condition, you should sit this one out, Katy?"

Lorne urged Katy to back up several feet. "It might be for the best, hon. I'm feeling queasy after seeing that. Lord knows how you must feel. Leave this to me."

Katy agreed, turning her back on the body, but continued to listen as she paced.

Once Katy had retreated and Lorne had prepared herself for the second reveal, Patti folded back the sheet once more. "So, the boat caught fire out at sea, I take it?"

"Yes, it did. If it was a simple case of this being a suspected accident, I wouldn't have invited you down here, Lorne."

"So what are we looking at, Patti? How do you know it isn't just an accident?"

"How many folks do you know who would be willing to shove a flare in their mouth and set it alight?"

"Umm… someone intent on committing suicide, perhaps?"

"Maybe. Not that I've ever seen anything like that used before, I hasten to add. However, that doesn't explain the wounds to the neck. Here." Patti pointed to the slits in the scorched flesh.

"How the heck did you spot that? There's hardly anything left of the head. Oh God, I think I'm going to puke."

Patti shot to her feet and turned Lorne by the shoulders. "Not over the body, young lady!"

The bile rose and settled in her throat instead of making an unwanted appearance. "I'm fine. False alarm. I'd rather not look at the corpse anymore, if you don't mind, just in case."

"That's understandable. Not everyone's stomach is as robust as mine. I just wanted you to be aware of the crime from the outset. I'm going to get the body transported to the lab now; thoroughly check it over for more wounds. I'll get the report back to you pronto."

"I'd appreciate that. Can you tell me more about where the boat was found?" Lorne asked, taking a tissue from her pocket. She wiped the beads of sweat from her brow.

"It was found anchored out at sea, just around the bay."

"So, if this is a murder case, then someone must have either boarded the boat from another vessel or gone out there with the deceased?"

"Possibly. Hold on." Patti walked over to one of the mechanics, and Lorne trailed her. "Do these boats usually come with some kind of additional craft that someone can use to come ashore if the boat gets into difficulty?"

Lorne laughed. "What my friend is trying to ask is whether a boat that size would have a dinghy aboard for emergencies?"

Patti sharply turned in her direction. "That's exactly what I said."

Lorne shook her head. "You didn't, but that's okay. I think the man understands now."

The mechanic rubbed his greasy hands on a cloth as he spoke. "The likelihood is yes, unless something major has gone wrong."

"Such as?" Lorne enquired.

"If there was a fire on the main vessel, any emergency craft might have been affected. Most of these cruisers come with inflatable dinghies. Inflatables don't do well when surrounded by heat."

"That's a good point. Thanks for the heads-up on that. It's a long shot, but do you recognise the boat at all?"

"Without a name, which has been burnt off, lady, it's difficult to tell one from another, especially when it's in that kind of condition."

"That's not exactly what I was hoping to hear. If I asked around the marina, do you think I might get a different answer?"

The mechanic hitched up his right shoulder. "Worth a shot."

Lorne and Patti retraced their steps back to the corpse. "The thing is, Lorne, just because the boat was tied up out in the bay, it doesn't mean that the victim was from around here. We're an island, with a very long coastline."

"I know. But we have to start somewhere, Patti, and around here is as good a place as any. When do you think Forensics will be able to get to a chassis number? Do boats even have a chassis number?"

"I'm not sure. They must have some form of identification aboard. I'll make sure they search for that first before they do anything else. How's that?"

"Perfect. Are you going to make a move now?"

"That's the plan. My guys are ready to transport the victim. I wanted you to see it first."

"I appreciate that, Patti. Katy and I will stick around here and start asking some questions. If the boat docked here, then someone must've noticed a stranger in town. There again, we're surmising the victim isn't local. We'll get the ball rolling until you can give us something positive to go on."

Lorne and Katy watched the pathology team load the body into the van and drive away. Patti waved as her vehicle followed her team away from the area. "Great. Where do we begin?" Lorne asked.

"Well, the mechanics don't appear to know anything, so I suppose we should start making enquiries with the other boats docked in the marina," Katy suggested.

"Do you want to split up or do this together?" Lorne asked, scanning the numerous boats moored up to the dock.

"Together would be best."

"Let's make a start, then."

"Can I make a suggestion," Katy asked tentatively.

Lorne's forehead wrinkled. "Of course. Go for it."

"If the boat departed from the marina, maybe it would be better to start where there's a gap, possibly vacated by a recent departure."

"Good idea. You get a gold star for that one, partner."

Katy smiled, the colour in her cheeks reverting to near normal after her icky spell in the mechanic's workshop.

They started at the far end of the marina and worked their way back towards the car park. All the jetties appeared to be reasonably full. It wasn't until they had travelled the length of the wooden structure that possible gaps between the boats became more apparent.

"Hello, ladies. You look lost. Can I help at all?" called out a man wearing shorts, a navy-blue windbreaker jacket, and a cap with an anchor at the front.

"You might be able to. Have you been moored here long?" Lorne asked.

"A few months. What do you need to know?"

Lorne and Katy produced their warrant cards. "I'm DI Lorne Warner, and this is DS Katy Foster. I presume you saw the incident with the boat out at sea that occurred yesterday. Any idea who the boat belonged to?"

The man chewed his lip and shook his head. "Dreadful incident. I heard the explosion. I guess that sort of thing happens once in a while with new vessels, Lord knows why."

"It was new? How do you know that, Mr...?"

"Sorry, Isaac Jacobs at your service, ladies."

Lorne nodded. "Pleased to meet you, Isaac. So you recognised the boat. Is that right?"

"Not really, miss. I tend to keep my eyes and ears open, though. Call me the neighbourhood watch patrol of the marina if you like. It's an unpaid role of course."

"Well, they're lucky to have your observational skills at their service. What else can you tell us, Isaac?"

The man in his early sixties vaulted sprightly off his boat and landed on the jetty beside them. "Well, the young guy arrived sometime yesterday morning. He started tinkering with his boat, his eyes constantly glued to the car park as if he was waiting for someone to arrive."

"I see. Did someone turn up?"

He clicked his tongue and scratched the side of his head. "They might have. I didn't really see. It was around lunchtime, you see." He rubbed his tummy. "If I don't feed the beast regularly, the ulcer, it plays up something chronic."

"So, was the boat still here when you resurfaced after lunch?" Lorne asked, disappointment clenching her stomach muscles.

"Unfortunately not."

"That's bad news. Do you think any of the other nearby boat owners would be able to assist us?"

"It was really quiet around here yesterday, what with it being a Sunday and all. Must be the time of the year. Most of these boats aren't touched now until the spring. I live on my boat all year round, hence me adopting the role of neighbourhood watch patrolman."

"What a shame. Can I ask if you caught the name of the boat? Or did you have a conversation with the boat owner perhaps? We're trying to ascertain if the owner was local or not."

"No, didn't catch the name of the boat. Silly of me, I know. I was building up to talk to the chap after lunch. Didn't want to pounce on him the minute he docked. You never know how folks are going to react. He might have thought I was just poking my nose into his business. I waved to him a few times to break the ice. He seemed pleasant enough, a little unsure of me to begin with, but then he was on the lookout for someone, like I said."

"In your considered opinion, do you think there was anything suspicious in his behaviour?" Lorne asked cagily.

"Suspicious? In what way?" He gasped as if cottoning on to her meaning. "A possible drug runner? Is that what you're getting at? My, oh my!"

Lorne chuckled and shrugged. "We have no idea about that at this present time. But the clues we have obtained so far are leading us down an unsavoury path. That's for sure."

"Unsavoury path, eh? Coppers' speak for suspicious goings on."

"You're very astute, Isaac. Can you point out any of the boat owners who might have witnessed the man's arrival at the marina?"

He pointed at a boat behind him. "There are a couple of young lads residing on that craft for the week. Rowdy most of the time, loud music, et cetera." He leaned forward and whispered, "Be glad to see the back of them come Friday, I can tell you. Even thought of anchoring this girl out at sea for the week, just to escape their racket and to get some decent kip."

"Which boat exactly?" Katy asked, looking over her shoulder.

"*The Dream Goddess*. I haven't seen them surface today as yet; far too early in the day for the likes of that mob. If they don't tone it down a bit, do I have your permission to call your mob and ask for backup? People need to respect other folks who live here permanently in search of peace and quiet."

"We'll have a quiet word with them about that. Don't worry. Is there anything else you can tell us about the boat in question?"

"No, sorry I couldn't be any more help. I take it the man didn't make it off the boat. Am I right?"

"You are, Isaac. Sadly, it looks like we're dealing with a murder enquiry."

"Whoa, the explosion was deliberate? The thought never even crossed my mind. That's incredible. I wish I'd been more observant in that case. It's this damn ulcer, gives me jip most of the time. Sorry, you don't want to hear about my aches and pains."

Lorne smiled sympathetically. "I hope you get your ulcer sorted soon. Thanks for your help. Have a good day."

The man reached out to shake their hands then hopped back on his boat. Lorne and Katy walked up the jetty and stopped outside *The Dream Goddess*.

"How do we wake them up?" Katy asked.

"No idea. I'll climb aboard and see if anyone surfaces."

"If they got rat-arsed last night, I reckon the odds on that happening are virtually zilch. Here, I'll help you."

Lorne held tightly to Katy's hand and gingerly climbed onto the boat's deck. She walked around in a circle, hoping her heels would be noisy enough to gain someone's attention. When no one surfaced, she knocked on the wooden door at the rear with a bar that was lying on the deck. *Nice! Good sense of security, I don't think.* "Hello, anyone there?"

A few moments later, a sleepy young man opened the door, wearing only a pair of boxer shorts. "Yeah, what do you want? We haven't ordered anything from anywhere."

Lorne flashed her ID inches before the man's eyes. "Can you see that clearly enough? My partner and I would like to ask you and your companions a few questions, once you're all dressed of course. We'll wait on the jetty. You have five minutes, okay?"

"About what? We haven't done anything wrong. Damn, is this about the party we had last night?"

Lorne issued the man a taut smile. "Four minutes and thirty seconds."

"Okay, okay I hear you."

Katy helped Lorne disembark the boat, and they both folded their arms and tapped a foot as they waited for the man and his shipmates to appear. Katy shuddered. "My feet are freezing. Hurry up, morons," she grumbled under her breath.

"Walk around a little. I agree—it is a little fresh. It's to be expected at this time of year. Here they are now. Glad they've seen sense and thrown on some clothes. I'd hate for their dicks to get frostbite," Lorne joked.

Katy turned her back on the men to laugh. "Did you have to say that? I'm going to have trouble keeping a straight face now."

Lorne winked at her and smiled at the three men lined up on the deck. "Morning, chaps. Sorry for the rude awakening. We're investigating a crime that took place yesterday in the vicinity and wondered if you'd be willing to help us with our enquiries."

The three men, varying in height and builds, all stared back at them, blank expressions on each of their unshaven faces. After a few seconds, the original man crossed his arms and said, "What sort of crime? I hope you're not suggesting we had anything to do with it? All we're guilty of is having a good time."

"A major crime is all I'm prepared to say right now. We've been told by one of your neighbours that you were present here yesterday. Is that right?"

"Yes, we had a lazy day. Listened to the match on the radio—Man City stuffed Man U, by the way—had a barbecue and a few beers to celebrate."

"Did you notice a new boat moored up close to Mr. Jacobs's boat over there?"

The main spokesperson shook his head and asked his companions, "Did you, guys?"

"Yes, you remember, Paul. Those two girls arrived," the cheeky-looking chappie with the slight beer belly replied.

Lorne turned to face Katy and raised an eyebrow. Katy took out her notebook.

Now that his memory had been jogged, the spokesperson clicked his fingers. "That's right. A couple of brunettes turned up. They looked up for a good time. Didn't they, boys?" He laughed and dug his elbows into the ribs of both of his companions, encouraging them to join in.

Lorne cleared her throat to gain their attention. "Good time? What exactly are you saying?"

The spokesperson lowered his hand to the top of his thighs. "Skirts up to here, stiletto heels, and bulging boobs in low-cut tops. The kind of getup girls wear when they're out on the pull."

"I see, and they got aboard the boat?"

"Yeah, I wolf whistled them as they passed, but they showed little interest, which kind of surprised me 'cause girls always fall for my outstanding charm and good looks." His friends tittered beside him like adolescent schoolboys.

Lorne tutted. "Okay, I know you're finding this a big joke, but do you mind restraining all the childish banter and just answering the questions properly?"

"Sorry. Carry on."

Lorne tried again. "Just to be clear, you say the women did get on the boat?"

"Yeah, the bloke who owned it—well, I assumed he owned it— ordered them, with a smile, to remove their shoes before getting on. Wise move, too, because they were killer heels."

Lorne cringed at the words. *Killer heels worn by killer women by all accounts!* "And they didn't protest?"

"Nope. Slipped them off, then the chap helped them board the boat one by one."

"Do you think they knew each other well?" Katy asked.

"Yeah, that's the impression I got. What about you, boys?"

"Yep, me, too," his shipmates agreed.

"Interesting. Did you keep an eye on them? After you initially showed interest in them, it would be hard for you not to watch the proceedings, right?"

"You're right. Discreetly, of course. Not that they hung around the marina for long. It was a matter of minutes before the boat left the jetty and slid out to sea."

"And everyone on the boat seemed to be having a good time? There was no shouting or confrontations from what you could see?"

Lorne asked, intrigued by the revelation that they might be looking at two female murderers who had carried out the crime.

"Yeah, they all seemed to be having a good time from what I could tell. One of the girls did appear a little sick once the engine started and the boat moved off, but apart from that, nothing out of the ordinary was going on."

"It must have been a boozy day for you if you didn't hear the explosion."

The three men looked at each other in confusion. "Explosion? What explosion?" the spokesman asked quietly, as if the reality of what had occurred had just struck him.

"The boat in question blew up around the coast and was hoisted out of the sea." Lorne stretched her neck to see if she could view the crane from where she was standing—she couldn't. Therefore, she doubted the men would have been aware of the charred boat sitting on the dock.

"Holy crap! What was it? A mechanical fault?"

"We're not sure yet. Our enquiries have only just commenced. Here's the thing—only one body was found aboard the boat when it was hauled back to shore."

"Really? One of the girls, or was it the bloke?"

"We have a male victim. No sign of either of the ladies at present. Of course, that's not to say that they won't show up within the next few days. They might have jumped overboard when the blaze started for all we know. We're just not sure right now. That's why we need to gather all the evidence we can find to help us build a case." Lorne didn't let on that the man had suffered fatal injuries to his neck.

"What about the emergency craft? Did the boat have a dinghy? Could the women have escaped using that?"

Lorne tilted her head. "May I ask what you do for a profession, Mr...?"

"It's Frankie Da Costa. I'm a trainee solicitor."

"Ahh... I understand now. Well, that's another angle that we're looking into, Mr. Da Costa. Is it too much to ask if you saw either of the women again later on that day?"

Da Costa shook his head. "Sorry, no, Inspector. We would have recognised those beauties in a heartbeat if they'd popped up again."

"Would you be willing to give a description to a police artist to help us identify the women?"

He scratched his head as he thought. "The mind is still a little fuzzy from the alcohol, but I'm sure we could come up with something for you to go on."

"That would be great. Will you be around the rest of the day?"

He nodded. "We hadn't made any plans for the day, had we, boys?"

"Just a touch of fishing, that's all," the cheeky one replied.

"Okay. I'll request a police artist to drop by and see you this afternoon. It would be really helpful if you can give us as much detail about these women as possible. Once we have your sketches to hand, we'll run a call for help through the media channels to see if anyone can identify the women."

"Anything we can do to help, we will. Sorry for all the messing about earlier. We truly didn't realise the gravity of the situation," Da Costa said, looking ashamed for their behaviour.

Lorne accepted his apology with a nod and a smile. "These things happen. I'll place a call now and let you know when to expect the artist. Thanks for your help. Oh, by the way, keep the noise down a little, and be respectful to the other people staying here, eh?"

The men nodded.

She and Katy bid the shocked men good day and walked back up the jetty. Lorne phoned the artist and arranged for the young woman to visit the men around four that afternoon. Before moving on to another jetty, Lorne ran back and relayed the information to the three men.

Lorne and Katy spent the next few hours going over the details of the three people they knew had been travelling on the boat with other boat owners in the marina, but nothing concrete in the way of extra evidence came their way.

CHAPTER FIVE

Claire sat in the drawing room of her luxurious art deco mansion alongside the open fire, where logs glowed brightly in its grate. Sighing, she picked disinterestedly at the prawn salad the housekeeper had prepared for her. *What has my life descended to all of a sudden? I need to look for a way out of all these mounting debts. If the girls ever found out the extent of my troubles, there would be hell to pay.*

The young Thai girl, she employed as a housekeeper, entered the room and bowed before her.

"Yes, Mai Ling? What is it?" she asked tersely.

"Telephone, madam. It's your daughter. She sound *vely* upset."

Claire's eyes fluttered shut, and she held out her hand to accept the phone. "Which one? I have four, remember?"

"Ah, solly. It is Miss Lucy." After giving Claire the phone, she walked backwards out of the room, still bent over at the waist.

Claire heaved out a sigh. Once upon a time, the housekeeper's quirky behaviour had endeared her to the woman. With all the financial strain she was under, the woman's simplistic ways and loyalty caused her nothing but irritation, like a lot of things lately. She held the phone up to her ear and heard her daughter's sobbing on the other end. *Here we go, yet another one of her little dramas to contend with.* "Hello, Lucy. How are you?"

"Oh, Mum, I don't know what to do."

"About what?" Claire snapped.

"Don't be like that, Mum. This is serious. Ryan hasn't come home," Lucy whined.

"So? He's probably off entertaining another of his clients," Claire offered, aware of where her son-in-law had been the day before.

"But he always rings me, never goes anywhere without sharing his schedule with me. He took off in the boat yesterday, and I haven't seen him since. It's so unlike him, Mum. What can I do? Is it too soon to ring the police?"

"No. Do *not* get them involved at this time. Give him another few hours to make contact. Have you tried calling his mobile?"

"Of course I have. I'm not thick."

"Don't shout at me, Lucy! It was a simple question," Claire retorted, the vein in her neck pulsing rapidly in anger. The door to the drawing room opened, and Teagan walked into the room. "I have to go, Lucy. Hang tight for a few hours. Ring his friends if you have to, but don't, for God's sake, ring the police."

"Okay. Sorry to intrude on your valuable time, Mother," her daughter shouted sarcastically before she hung up.

Claire ended the call and threw the phone on the Queen Anne winged chair behind her. "That was Lucy. What the fuck have you done, Teagan? I can see the devilment and defiance lurking in your eyes."

Teagan shrugged. "As requested, Helen and I retrieved the papers."

"And why are you turning up now to tell me this? I expected you back yesterday. I can sense when you're keeping things from me. Lucy is beside herself. What have you done to Ryan?"

Teagan threw herself into the two-seater chesterfield sofa, placed her arms along the back of the chair, and crossed her long slender legs at the same time. "You gave us strict instructions to get the deeds. Helen and I have done just that."

"At what bloody cost? Stop toying with me, girl. What have you done?"

"You know as well as I do, he was spinning out of control. I dealt with his crappy attitude once and for all."

Claire's eyes widened with rage. "I'm going to say this one last time, and this time I want the truth. Where is Ryan?"

Teagan looked down the length of her arm and studied the diamond ring on her hand before she spoke again. Her reply was riddled with venom: "He had every intention of going back on his word. I needed to prevent that. People, outsiders, need to realise that we won't be messed with."

"You're insane! He wasn't an outsider. He was a pivotal part to our plans. Jesus, why is it when I let you loose on things, it always goes belly up? You're a bloody nightmare to deal with at times, Teagan. You think you know what's best, but you're simply delusional."

"That's what you think, Mother. He was about to jump ship. Excuse the pun. Did you know he'd recently spent forty grand on that boat?"

"So what? It was his money. What gives you the right to say what people in this family can spend their money on?" Claire shot out of the chair and paced up and down on the newly fitted Axminster carpet in front of her daughter.

"Taking a leaf out of your book, Mother dearest. You've been telling us all for years what to do, and not to do, with our money."

"*You're* the one who is out of control, Teagan. I thought marrying Lee would tame you. If anything, it's made you sodding worse. You're becoming uncontrollable. Where are the papers?"

"Ah… the reality has suddenly sunk in, has it? They're safe," Teagan replied smugly.

"What do you mean they're *safe*?"

Teagan shrugged. "They're safe, and they're going to remain in my care. Call it insurance, if you like."

Claire stopped pacing and swiftly turned. She lowered herself to within inches of her daughter's face. "Stop testing me, Teagan. There's only ever going to be one winner if you tangle with me, girl. If you haven't learnt that over the years, then shame on you."

"Your threats mean fuck all to me, Mother. You're losing your hold over this family. Surely you can see that?"

"I might be in my sixties, but I can still outwit you, my girl."

Teagan's lips parted to show her gleaming, recently whitened teeth. "You've trained me well, Mother. Maybe it's time you stepped aside and let me take over the reins."

"Never! Not while there's still a breath left in my body. You screw up too frequently for the others to put their trust in you. This family will never prosper under your leadership," Claire raged, standing upright to combat the pain in her spine from bending over for so long.

"I already have Helen on my side. She's fed up with being ordered around by you. She told me as much yesterday."

"Liar! If that really is true, then she should have the guts to tell me that herself. Now, what have you done to Ryan? I told you to get the papers from him—that was all."

"We had to do something drastic. He had no intention of handing over those papers. I got the feeling he had plans to use them against us. I had to stop him."

Claire lowered herself into the chair and swept a hand over the beads of sweat breaking out on her brow. "I've had your sister, Lucy on the phone, looking for him. Are you telling me that she'll never see him again?"

Teagan laughed. "Oh, she'll see him all right, in a mortuary fridge."

"What the hell have you done, Teagan?" Claire held her head in her hands for a moment or two. When she glanced in her daughter's direction again, Teagan was grinning, looking very pleased with herself. Claire's stomach twisted as she sensed her own end looming. *How do I combat the spitting image of myself? I've moulded her into this monster. How do I now battle her will and succeed?*

CHAPTER SIX

"One last try before we call it a day, eh?" Lorne winked at Katy as her partner shook her head.

"That's what you bloody said half an hour ago. My feet are like blocks of ice. I'll be waddling like a penguin soon."

Lorne dipped her hand into her jacket pocket and produced a bunch of keys. She held them out to Katy. "Here, you go and sit in the car while I talk to this couple," she said, motioning with her head in the direction of an elderly man and woman, sitting under a rug on a small yacht.

Katy gave her a long-suffering smile. "I'm sorry to wimp out on you."

"Nonsense, you need to take care of the baby. I won't be long."

Lorne watched Katy safely leave the jetty, then approached the last boat in this section of the marina. "Ahoy there. Any chance I can have a quick chat?"

"Hello, dear. Do you want to come aboard?" The elderly gentleman threw back the tartan rug and rushed to the back of the boat to lend Lorne a hand.

Once she was on the deck, Lorne showed the couple her warrant card and explained why she was there.

"Oh my, that's awful. Harold, I think I remember seeing that boat yesterday on its journey out to sea."

"That's right. You commented on the girls' appearance, said it was far too cold to be dressed like that in December, especially venturing out on such a choppy sea."

Lorne's spirits rose with the news. "Brilliant! I don't suppose you got a look at the name of the boat? Or did you recognise any of the passengers as locals? We're trying to establish if the boat was from around here or somewhere farther up the coast."

Harold chewed on his lip for a moment or two. "I definitely saw the name. Bugger me if I can recall what it was, though. Bloody memory always fails me at the wrong time. How about you, Sylvia, can you remember what it was called?" he asked his wife.

Sylvia, cradling a cup between her hands, shook her head slowly. "I'm sorry. No, I can't."

"Wait a minute, now don't laugh when I say this, but I have an idea it was something nautical." Harold looked excited that he'd managed to summon up the information from some kind of an abyss in his mind.

"Well, that could prove to be helpful, eventually," Lorne said, chuckling.

"I tried. I suppose without knowing who the boat belongs to, you're going to have trouble getting in touch with the next of kin," Harold suggested.

"Exactly. It's certainly making life difficult for us at the moment. I'm sure something in the line of clues will come our way soon. Thanks for your help anyway. Enjoy the rest of your day, both of you."

Disappointed, Lorne hopped back onto the jetty and returned to the car.

"Anything?" Katy asked when Lorne jumped in behind the steering wheel.

"Not really. The gent thought the name of the boat was something nautical. He couldn't be any more accurate than that."

"There's a novelty—a boat with a nautical name." Katy laughed.

"Granted, it's not the best clue in the world, but it's better than a piss in the ocean." Lorne started the engine and drove out of the car park. "They also gave a similar description of the three people who boarded the boat. Let's hope something comes from the sketch artist's jaunt down here later, because as it stands, we have very little to go on until Patti and her team either send us the results of the postmortem or manage to locate the chassis number, if it has one."

"Do you know if the media have put this out yet? They're usually quick off the mark when something of this magnitude takes place. It's not every day a boat explodes off the Kent coastline," Katy said when they were caught up in a slow-moving queue of traffic.

"I'll leave you to check on that when we return. If the answer is no, can you organise a slot to hit the news tonight? On second thoughts, *I'll* do that. I hope it's not putting too much pressure on the artist to complete her job quickly. I'll have a word, see what she says."

"I've just had a thought."

"About what?" Lorne asked, turning to face her partner.

"What if the boat is owned by a foreigner? That's going to make it nigh impossible to come up with an identification, isn't it?"

"I have no idea how these things work. Let's see what AJ can find out for us when we get back. I would've thought once we have a chassis number, or the equivalent, then there would be a worldwide registration network set up—you'd like to think there was anyway. This is all a little out of our field of expertise at this point. I hope that doesn't prove to be detrimental to the case. Someone out there is missing a husband or a boyfriend. Maybe it won't be long before that person comes forward."

"If they are, then it's likely, by what we've been told already, that the victim had a penchant for the ladies, which in the long run, has probably led to his downfall."

When they arrived back at the station, they were in a race against time to get the tasks they'd discussed in the car into action before the end of the shift.

Lorne spoke to her contact at the TV station, who said she'd heard about the incident but hadn't garnered enough information to think it warranted a slot on the news. She asked Gemma if she would be willing to run the story within the next twenty-four hours once the sketches became available. The answer was a categorical yes. Before heading home that evening, Lorne checked in with Patti. It was always good to keep in contact with the pathologist at the beginning of a case.

"Any news, Patti?"

"Eager, aren't you? I completed the PM about an hour ago. I'm still waiting for news on trying to find the boat ID for you."

"Talking of IDs, I don't suppose the victim had anything on him, such as a wallet?"

"If only. The PM verified that he was dead before the explosion and thankfully before the flare was lit."

"So, someone intentionally tried their hardest to make it difficult to ID this man, is that your assumption?" Lorne asked, tapping her pen against her chin.

"Yes, that's my professional opinion at this time. Did you manage to gain anything from your enquiries?"

"A number of witnesses have told us that two women turned up at the marina and boarded the boat. It all seemed friendly enough from what they could tell."

"Strange that the boat only ventured out a short way before the attack took place."

Lorne nodded as if Patti were sitting in the room with her. "Very strange. Maybe they were prioritising their escape plan from the get-go. Pure conjecture at this point. So, are you telling me that you think the victim died from the fatal wound to his neck as you predicted at the marina?"

"Either that or the wound to the heart via the wound to his back. It's hard to tell which came first and which wound ultimately ended the man's life. I know one thing for definite—the offender's anger was evident in the attack. Is a woman capable of overcoming a man of his size easily? I'm not sure about that, but the intervention of alcohol might have aided the attack."

"Interesting. Don't forget there were two women. All right, Patti, I'm about to call it a day here. Will you ring me as soon as you have an ID for the boat?"

"Of course. Have a good evening, Lorne. Think of me slicing open yet another three bodies before the end of my shift, won't you?"

"God, I'd rather not. I think Tony mentioned he was planning on knocking up liver and onions for dinner."

Lorne could still hear Patti's laughter as she hung up. She looked up to find a wincing Katy leaning against the doorframe. "You really eat that stuff?"

"Hey, it's good for you. You should try it. It would be beneficial for the baby, too."

"I'd rather stick bloody cocktail sticks in my eyes," Katy replied, cringing.

Lorne chuckled. "That was Patti. No news on the boat ID as yet. She's going to chase it up tomorrow. I think we should call it a day now, don't you?"

"Yep. I need to get home and soak in the bath. My feet still haven't thawed out yet."

"Poor you. Get AJ to give you a foot massage to get the circulation going again."

Katy turned on her heels and waved goodbye over her shoulder. Lorne finished dealing with a few important papers she needed to get back to the chief pronto, then she headed home for the evening herself.

A strange car was sitting in the driveway of the kennels when she arrived home. She walked into the house to find Charlie, Tony, and a young man in his twenties sitting around the kitchen table. Two dogs—Sheba the German shepherd and a Border collie not dissimilar in colour to Lorne's old dog, Henry—sniffed each other inquisitively.

"Hello, you must be Brandon." Lorne held out her hand to shake the young man's.

He rose from his chair, which gave him top marks for having good manners. "Pleased to meet you, Mrs. Warner."

"Well, that makes me feel ancient. Just plain old Lorne will do."

He smiled awkwardly and apologised.

"And who is this little beauty?" She knelt on the floor, forgetting that she was wearing her best suit, and stroked the collie.

"This is Tess, the star of the agility club, Mum. Or should I say the present star, until Sheba steals the show," Charlie joked, beaming at her new fella.

Both Tess and Sheba enjoyed the attention heaped upon them for the next few minutes, then Lorne stood up and washed her hands at the sink before joining the others at the table. "I can't smell any dinner, husband dearest."

"That's because I haven't had a chance to create anything yet. I've had a hell of a day. Tell you about it later. I thought we might get fish and chips. Would that be okay?"

"Of course. Will you be joining us, Brandon? You're more than welcome to."

"Can I take a rain check on that, Mrs… er, I mean, Lorne? I said I'd help Dad at the club tonight, to set up for the class."

"Oh, you work at the agility club? I didn't realise that."

"I help out occasionally. Dad and I run a plumbing business."

"That's handy to know for when we spring a leak," Lorne quipped.

"Mum, did you have to?" Charlie complained.

Lorne tweaked her daughter's cheek. "What? Am I embarrassing you, dear child?"

Charlie's eyes rolled up to the ceiling. "I give up. I just wish you would do the same," she grumbled. "Come on, Brandon, we'll give Sheba and Tess a run in the paddock before you leave." Charlie tucked her chair under the table.

Poor Brandon wasn't sure what to do. His head swivelled between Lorne and Charlie. Lorne grabbed her daughter's wrist and pulled her to stand alongside her, draping an arm around her daughter's waist. "You'll get used to us soon, Brandon. Charlie hates me winding her up."

"I keep telling you, Mum, I'm a grown woman now."

"As you can see, she gives as good as she gets."

"Leave the youngsters alone, Lorne. Our fish and chips are calling. Are you having any before you shoot off, Charlie?"

"Too bloody right, I am."

Tony, Charlie, and Brandon along with the two dogs, left the kitchen. Lorne busied herself setting the table for dinner while her mind churned over the mysterious case she'd been working on all day. The most annoying part of her job had to be when she was presented with a John Doe to identify. On this occasion, the John Doe seemed to be a wealthy one.

The ringing phone interrupted her train of thought. She answered it in the lounge and flopped onto the sofa. "Hey, sis, I was going to ring you later."

"You were? That'd be a first," Jade snapped back unnecessarily.

Lorne cringed. It had been a while since she'd rung her sister to see how she was coping. Since losing their father over five years ago, Jade had been under the doctor's care for extreme stress and insomnia issues. Lorne felt the nick of the blade from the guilt knife Jade jabbed at her heart. "How are you?"

"No change. I'm ringing up to say we're off to Italy for Christmas. I'm calling to see if you want to exchange presents before we go or after if you want to leave it until we get back in January."

"Damn, I haven't even thought about Christmas yet."

"Now there's a surprise," Jade mumbled just loud enough for Lorne to hear.

"Don't start, Jade. You know what my life is like and how hectic it is."

"Yeah, me, me, and me. That's all that matters to you, isn't it, Lorne? Well, what about what *I* want? I need my sister to take time out for *me*. To pick up the phone every now and again to ask how I'm doing, but no, you're always too damn busy."

"Jade, where's all this coming from? The last thing I want, or need, is to fall out with you. I know you're still smarting from losing Dad. I miss him a great deal, too, you know."

"Do you? Not as much as I do."

"It's not a competition, Jade, and I refuse to revisit this conversation every time you lose yet another night's sleep."

"You know what, Lorne—why don't I stop ringing you altogether? No, I'll go one better… I'll move to a different country, and then I'll be out of your hair for good. How's that?"

"What are you talking about? For goodness' sake, Jade, I ring when I have the time. I work full time and then come home here and have to help out at the kennels." The last part was a bit of a fib, and Lorne cringed again when Jade pulled her up on it.

"Liar! Charlie and Tony look after the dogs, not you. I'm going to hang up now before I say something I regret." And she did just that.

Lorne held the phone away from her ear and shook it angrily. "You mean you haven't already? Jesus, woman, give me a break, please?"

"That's the first sign."

Lorne held a hand over her chest when she heard Tony's voice at the door of the lounge. "You scared the bloody shit out of me."

"Who was on the phone?"

Lorne followed him back into the kitchen and removed the warm plates she'd placed in the oven after he'd left. "Jade. I can never do anything right in her eyes. She's threatening to move to another country."

"You know she always strikes out when she wants to let off steam, hon. Just ignore her."

"That's getting exceedingly hard to do. Why does she always take her foul moods out on me? It hurts so much. We used to be close once upon a time, believe it or not. Since Dad's death, it's like she regards me as some kind of enemy."

"Do you think she blames you?"

"No more than I blame myself. We all thought he was on the road to recovery when he passed away. Hey, it wasn't my fault that Katy and I got kidnapped that day. I'll always feel guilty for the stress I caused him. She understands that, doesn't she? She should do. Anyway, she brought up the 'C' word."

Tony's eyes bulged. "What? Cancer?"

Lorne bit her lip. "No, sorry. Christmas. She asked if we wanted to exchange presents before or after the festivities as they're going to Italy this year."

"You haven't even started buying gifts, have you?"

"Nope. I never tend to buy until the very last week. Maybe we can go shopping at the weekend, all being well?"

"Why not?"

Lorne hugged him and kissed him on the lips. "What would I do without you?"

"I ask myself the same thing every day."

She pushed away from him and narrowed her eyes. "Hmm… you do, do you? That's pretty magnanimous of you, Mr. Warner."

CHAPTER SEVEN

"You look rough," Katy observed as she climbed out of her car.

"And there was me thinking you were a mate," Lorne complained.

"Oops… a foul mood to boot. I sense someone has had a bout of family trouble since leaving work yesterday."

"You're too cute for your own good. You'd be right of course. Just feeling a little sorry for myself after my lovely sister called me selfish."

"What? Why? You're anything but. Is she still on those happy pills from the doc?"

In spite of feeling miserable, Lorne found herself laughing at Katy's question. "Yeah, the doc is still prescribing. The problem is that folks forget how much the body gets used to the drugs after a while and how ineffective they become. I've never really been one for popping pills for that very reason."

"I can understand that. Maybe she should try seeing another shrink. I know her last experience seeking out professional advice along those lines didn't end well, but not every psychiatrist turns out to be a serial killer."

"I'll be sure to add that tagline when I suggest it to her—not." They walked into the station and made their way upstairs. Lorne noticed that Katy held her stomach once or twice during the journey. "Is there something you need to share with me?"

"Not really. Babies kick periodically, according to my doc. I've just got to get used to it. I wish this little guy would give the soccer routine a rest now and then. It would go a long way to making this pregnancy more bearable."

"Really? Can I have a feel?"

Katy offered Lorne access to her increasing bulge. Just as Lorne held her hand in place, Chief Roberts appeared behind them.

"Haven't you got work to do, ladies?" he asked sharply.

Lorne yanked her hand away and continued to climb the stairs as she mumbled, "Morning to you too, Mr. Grouchy."

Ignoring her comment, Sean asked, "Are you busy this morning, Lorne?"

"It depends. You tell me what you want to see me about, and then I'll decide."

"Ever the wise arse. I wanted to run through a possible windfall coming the station's way soon and would like your insight on where you think the funds would be best suited."

They reached the top of the stairs. "I have a few things I need to check out first thing. I can come and see you around elevenish. How's that?"

"Perfect. I'll see you then."

Katy and Lorne watched him walk towards his office.

"Well, that was weird. Does he usually ask your opinion on such matters?" Katy asked.

"Nope. Very weird indeed. Unless he was using that as an excuse to see me of course."

"For what reason?"

"I don't know. I seem to be everyone's very own agony aunt lately. Let's leave the assumptions there. We have work to do. I want to press on with the case this morning. Roberts is bound to ask how we're progressing with it."

Some of the team, including AJ, were already at their computers. "Morning, all. Anything of interest develop overnight?"

Karen raised her hand.

Lorne walked across the room to speak to her.

"Morning, boss. I did have one interesting call from a taxi driver." She searched the desk for her notes. "He saw the bulletin on the news regarding the boat fire and contacted us. He said he was on duty when the fire happened and picked up two women around that time."

"Intriguing. Did he say where he dropped them off?"

"He couldn't give any more details than that, except that he was asked to drive them to the car park at the marina."

"Okay, well that's something, I suppose. AJ can you check any CCTV footage relating to the area around that time, please?"

"Is it worth paying this driver a visit?" Katy asked.

"Stephen, are you up for taking a statement this morning? Actually, on second thoughts, ring the taxi firm and see when the driver is on shift, will you? Maybe you can call round and see him at home. That'll be better."

"I'll get on it first thing, boss."

"At the moment, it's all we have to go on until the chassis number comes our way from SOCO. I'll be in my office." Lorne grabbed a coffee at the machine and settled behind her desk to do battle with her endless mind-numbing paperwork.

At around ten thirty, the phone broke her momentum of tearing through and signing numerous forms. "DI Lorne Warner."

"Lorne, it's Patti. I have the next piece of the puzzle for you."

"The chassis number?" Lorne's slouch was a thing of the past as her interest piqued. "That's brilliant news. Hopefully, it is. Don't tell me that you've only got half the number?"

"Ah, you know me so well."

"Damn!"

"I'm teasing you. No, it's intact and very legible."

"Excellent news. Fire away."

Patti reeled off the number, and Lorne jotted it down in her notebook. "You're amazing. Thanks for rushing it through for me. Let's hope it'll help us identify the victim."

"Let me know if and when you get a name, and I can do the necessary to match any dental records et cetera to make a formal ID."

"Of course. Thanks, Patti. Speak soon." Lorne bolted out of her office and rushed over to AJ's desk. "I have the chassis number, AJ. Want me to pass it on to someone else while you continue with the CCTV observations?"

"No. I can do both, boss. Give me half an hour."

"Okay." She spun round and told Katy, "I might as well see what Roberts wants now. I'll be on tenterhooks around here otherwise."

Katy nodded. "Good luck."

Lorne knocked on Roberts's door after his PA gave her the all-clear.

"Enter," his voice boomed.

Lorne walked in and sat opposite Sean. "You wanted to see me, sir?"

"It was a ruse."

"A ruse?" Lorne frowned.

"I really wanted to know how you think Katy is coping. I was a little perplexed observing the pair of you this morning. I don't have to remind you that you're both supposed to be professional career women."

"The baby kicked. I'm disappointed in you, Sean. How can you say either Katy or myself never take our jobs seriously?"

He reclined in his chair, eyes sparkling with something Lorne found hard to fathom. "You're putting words into my mouth, Lorne. Not once did I say you never take your jobs seriously. I'm concerned. Forgive me for caring. Not many chiefs would."

"I'm sorry. I shouldn't have bitten your head off. Anyway, Katy is still one hundred percent capable of carrying out her normal duties. I'll let you know when I think she isn't. How's that? I'd hate for you to be holed up in this office, contemplating if she was fit for the role or not."

"There you go again, trying to twist my concerns into a problem. Okay, now that's sorted, don't let me hold you up."

"Thanks. I need to get on, as the pathologist has rung to give me something important regarding our latest case."

"What's that?"

"The one piece of information that we're hoping will help us ID the victim."

"You better get back to it in that case. Keep me informed, on both counts, all right?"

"I'll do that."

Lorne left the office to return to the incident room, which was buzzing with excitement. "You've come up with the goods, I take it?" She approached AJ, who was triumphantly waving a piece of paper at her.

"Ryan Timcott. The boat was based in Horning, Norfolk."

"Excellent news. Let's see what facts we can dig up about Mr. Timcott before we make contact with any relatives. Usual details. We need to tread carefully if he turns out to have a wife, bearing in mind the fact that witnesses have told us that two women were aboard his boat."

"Maybe one of them was his wife," Katy said with a shrug.

"Perhaps you're right. I can't see it myself, Katy."

Lorne pulled up a chair next to AJ. He was the whizz with computers, and he managed to find the most significant piece of information they needed to take the case forward.

"I have his address, or should I say *addresses*. One here in Fulham and the other in Horning, Norfolk. According to the electoral role, he's married to a Lucy Timcott and registered at both addresses."

"Excellent news. Fancy taking a trip out to Fulham, Katy?"

"Why not?"

The residence they arrived at was huge.

"Why am I not surprised to find out he's this wealthy?"

"I guess the boat was a giveaway," Katy offered.

Lorne rang the bell located in the centre of the large oak door, and it echoed around the inside of the house. "Damn. Looks like there's nobody at home. No cars on the drive, nothing."

"Wouldn't a place this size need some kind of staff, be it a housekeeper or someone along those lines?"

"Maybe she's out on a shopping trip. I don't know. Perhaps this is the holiday home and the main residence is the house in Norfolk."

"Maybe. I know that look. Don't tell me you're intending on going up there to find out."

Lorne sniggered. "Nope. Too far for us to travel and out of our jurisdiction."

"We need a contact in the Norfolk Constabulary. Any suggestions?"

A lightbulb went off in Lorne's head. "Actually, I do. Back to the station."

"Well, don't leave me in suspense. Who?"

"My old friend Sally Parker. She's a detective inspector. We went through our inspector training together at Hendon. I've been meaning to catch up with her. Not spoken to her for a few months, might even be years. You know how time flies." Lorne poked a card through the letterbox of the house instructing Mrs. Timcott to contact her ASAP. Then they returned to the station.

Lorne flicked open her address book and dialled Sally's mobile number.

"Hello, DI Sally Parker."

"Sally? Guess who this is?"

There was silence on the other end of the line for a moment or two. Lorne sensed the cogs turning in Sally's mind and heard her old friend tut. "Is that you, Lorne?"

"Bingo. How the devil are you? It's been ages since we chatted."

"It has. Up and down, you know how it is? To what do I owe the pleasure?"

"Sorry to be blunt—it is about work, I'm ashamed to say. It's been on my mind to call you for months, but…"

"No need to apologise. I'm in the same line of business, remember? I completely understand. What can I do for you?"

"We're investigating a murder enquiry. We thought it was a mere accident to begin with, but it soon escalated into more."

"Sounds intriguing. How does this concern me?"

"The murder victim is registered to two addresses: one down here in London, the other up there on your patch. The investigation is still in its infancy, so we don't have much to go on at present. However, we're aware of at least two other people who we're interested in chatting to, shall we say?"

"Do you want to give me the victim's name?"

"Ryan Timcott. Does it ring any bells?" Lorne asked, more out of hope than expectation.

"Nope, nothing is coming to mind. Why don't you fill me in on what you have so far?"

Lorne brought her up to date on what they had gleaned so far. "That's it really."

"And you have no idea who these two women are?"

"Not at this point, no."

"So, we'll need to tread very carefully where the wife is concerned. Is that what you're saying?"

"Exactly, Sally. Hey, one of the women might have been her for all we know."

"Do you want me to go to the address to break the news in person?"

"I'm not sure. As the case seems to be quite complex, I'd like to do that myself if possible."

"You mean that you're as much a control freak as me and you'd rather not relinquish your hold on the case."

Lorne laughed. "I see your memory is still A1. I seem to recall we had the same trait in that respect, during our training. Both stubborn and neither of us willing to be easily put off the scent by criminals."

"That's still the case with me."

Lorne's mind went into overdrive as a plan began to form. *Dare I ask? To even suggest such a thing without running it past the chief first? Bugger it, I'm going to do it.*

"Are you still there, Lorne?"

"Sorry. Yes, I'm still here. You know me of old, so I'm going to come straight to the point."

"Would it be better for me to sit down for this?"

"That's up to you. What about if I drove up there and we visited Lucy Timcott together? Would you be up for that?"

"Christ, you don't do anything by half, do you?"

"Tell me if you think it's an absurd idea. The last thing I want to do is step on your toes. You know me; I tend to go on gut instinct, and there's just something about this case that's prodding me to go the extra mile. Not only that, it would be great to see you after all these years."

"Why not? It would be brilliant to catch up. Why don't you bring hubby with you? You can spend the weekend with me and my folks. You remember them, right? They'd love to see you, too."

"Crikey, you're as bad as me. Once an idea takes hold it gets carried along at the speed of an express train. I'll have to check with Tony first. If he's agreeable, we could drive up tomorrow. How's that? It's not exactly the weekend, but I suppose the sooner we tell the victim's wife, the better."

Sally yelped with excitement. "Bloody marvellous. I do believe you've just made my week."

Lorne smiled. It was wonderful to hear her friend so excited at the prospect of them meeting up again. She was sure that Tony would have no hesitation about agreeing to the adventure, too, although she wasn't sure Chief Roberts or Katy would feel the same way once she broke the news to them. "Can I confirm everything later this evening, Sally? I'll have to pick the right moment to broach the subject with the chief."

"Of course, you've got my mobile number. Call when ready. You'll have to take us as you find us, if that's okay?"

"Of course." Lorne ended the call then immediately rang Tony's mobile. He answered the call after two rings. "Busy?"

"We're on a stakeout. What's up?"

"I won't keep you for long. Any chance you can take the next couple of days off?"

"It's doable. Why?"

Lorne ran through the conversation she'd had with Sally and waited for him to respond. She looked down at her fingers and almost laughed when she saw them tightly crossed.

"Sounds like fun. I'll run it past Joe. Gotta go. See you later."

He ended the call before she could say anything else. Lorne left the office to find Katy. "Umm... I might be going on a trip."

Katy looked puzzled by the out-of-the-blue announcement. "Where to?"

"Norfolk, would you believe?"

"For the case? You think it warrants a special trip, Lorne?"

"I won't know until I get there. I think it warrants the personal touch—*my* personal touch. You know what I'm like, Katy. I don't want to hear things second-hand. Did I sound convincing?"

"What does that mean?"

"I'm going to need Sean to give me the go-ahead. You can handle things at this end. I'll only be away for a day or two at the most."

Katy shrugged. "There's only one way to find out, and yes, we're more than capable as a team of working on our own initiative in your absence."

"I know that. It wasn't meant as a slight against any of you. You know me better than that, Katy."

"Shoo… go and tell the chief."

Lorne needn't have worried about Sean's reaction to her request. He thought it was a great idea, and she got the impression he would have volunteered to go with her, had it not been for the mammoth proportions of the paperwork piled high on his desk. She had an inkling that his role in the last two cases the team had solved had sparked into life his need to get away from the constraints of sitting behind his desk, dealing with mind-numbing paperwork day in, day out. She cringed at the thought of having Sean within close proximity, questioning every move or thought she made during a case. She was grateful his workload was keeping him tied to the desk.

He let her go with his best wishes but ordered her to return within forty-eight hours. Lorne neglected to tell her boss that Tony was accompanying her. She had a feeling he wouldn't have been too impressed by that snippet of news.

CHAPTER EIGHT

Once they eventually found their way off the M25, the journey to the east coast was a pleasant one. Even though they had left the house early, the whole population of the capital appeared to have had the same idea about getting away for a few days that morning. When they hit the A11, they were able to breathe far easier. Lorne had asked Tony to drive because she loathed the congestion that often took place on the M25. Tony breathed a sigh of relief when he pulled into the police station car park at Wymondham around ten thirty.

Lorne flashed her warrant card at the female officer on duty behind the reception desk. "We're here to see DI Sally Parker."

"Take a seat, ma'am. I'll see if she's available."

Seconds later, the inner door buzzed, and Sally, who was still sporting the same blonde hairstyle, and looked as if she hadn't gained a single ounce of fat since their final meeting at Hendon a few years back, swept into the room. She rushed up to Lorne and hugged her so tightly that Lorne almost choked as the air rushed out of her lungs.

"It's so fabulous to see you," Sally said, finally releasing her.

Lorne coughed. "You, too, despite the damage you've done to my insides."

Sally slapped Lorne's upper arm. "Get on with you. It would take more than a friendly hug to knock the wind out of a tough bird like you," Sally jested.

Tony cleared his throat and held out his hand. "And I'm her other half, Tony Warner. Pleased to meet you, Sally. When we have a spare five minutes, you can dish the dirt on what my darling wife got up to in her training days."

The pair shook hands, and Sally winked at him. "Impossible, Tony, not because we made a secret pact never to divulge such stories, but because you'd need to stick around for at least a month before we even broke the surface."

"Hey, you! Don't go saying that. Knowing my husband, he'll think you're bloody serious."

The three of them laughed. Sally signed Lorne and Tony in as visitors and issued them both with passes, then they all ascended the stairs to her office, where Sally proudly introduced her visitors to the team. "Coffee first, then we'll visit the victim's wife. Is that okay with you, Lorne?"

"Sure. We're totally in your hands. Have you managed to find out anything about the victim?"

"Nothing much. Let's see what today brings and go from there. I have to say, I'm getting the same kind of niggle that you have about this case. Something doesn't ring true," Sally called out from her position by the vending machine.

"It's strange. Maybe I should have called my psychic friend, Carol, before we headed up here. Just to see what she saw, if anything."

Sally returned, carrying two cups of coffee, shaking her head. "I can't believe you still have faith in all that claptrap. I would've thought you'd grown out of it by now."

Lorne glanced at Tony, who was smirking. "Go on, tell her. You believe in Carol's abilities, too, now, don't you?"

Tony placed his cup on the desk behind him and raised his hands. "I admit I used to be a total sceptic until Carol proved her worth. Every now and again, she missed the mark, but just lately, her psychic powers have helped Lorne—and me, I have to admit—solve some major crimes. In fact, if it hadn't been for Carol's input into Lorne's last case, I doubt Lorne would still be with us or in this country."

"Really? How come?" Sally perched her backside on the desk behind her.

"It's a long story. Basically, Carol had a vision of where the person who had abducted me was holding me captive. It happened to be a small airport. If Tony and his partner—oh, and Sean, my chief—hadn't rescued me, I would more than likely be ingrained in the sex trade by now, along with my daughter, Charlie."

Sally seemed shocked by the revelation. "Whoa, you're having me on, aren't you?"

Lorne shook her head. "Totally true." She leaned over and kissed her husband on the cheek. "My hero saved me from an inevitable life of torture and slavery." Lorne shuddered at the image her words conjured up.

"I had no idea." Sally raised her coffee cup. "To heroes. Where would we be without them?"

Lorne tweaked Tony's face as the colour rose in his cheeks. "I'd definitely be lost without mine." Lorne eyed her friend with concern as a shadow of sadness descended. She took a few steps closer to Sally. "One day, you'll find a fella who is worth sharing your life with, hon. Never give up hope. Don't let the bitterness of your past relationship cast clouds over your future. You're too strong to let one man cause a lifetime of damage to your heart and your head. Seriously, I thought I was stuck for life in a dead-end marriage to Charlie's dad, but the minute I met Tony, I knew that I'd spend the rest of my life with him."

Sally's eyes misted over. "Did Tony realise that, too?"

Tony winked at Sally. "What can I say, Sally? She's a convincing woman."

Lorne laughed. "Romantic *isn't* his middle name, either." She watched Sally intently for a few minutes as her friend churned what Lorne had said through her mind. Unexpected expressions flowed across Sally's face. Lorne held out a hand for Sally to grasp, and she whispered, "I know that look. You've met someone already, haven't you?"

Sally's eyes widened. She scanned the room to see if any members of her team had overheard their conversation, then she placed a finger to her lips. "I don't know. It might be one-sided. Who can tell with these things? Let's get back on terra firma and stick to the case instead, eh?"

Lorne agreed. "Is the victim's house far from here?"

"Not too far. I sent one of the boys out to the residence to see if someone was around. He reported back that he saw two cars at the residence."

"And when was this?" Lorne asked, her interest piqued.

"Around nine this morning."

"I'm even keener to get out there now." Lorne downed the remains of her coffee and urged Sally and Tony to do the same. "Time's a-wasting, peeps."

Outside in the car park, they agreed they should all pile into Sally's car. Her partner, Jack, decided to remain at the station to continue delving into the victim's past with the rest of the team.

Sitting directly on the bank of the River Bure was a timber-framed building with its own mooring and boathouse.

Tony whistled. "Nice gaff."

"Something I'm guessing we'd only be able to afford in our dreams," Lorne said, twisting in her seat to look at him.

"You're not wrong there. Can you imagine what this place would be worth if it was situated on the Thames?"

"Maybe that's why they own a mansion in Fulham and a stunning riverside retreat in Norfolk," Lorne suggested.

Sally smiled. "You're missing out on a lot living down there, Lorne."

"Story of our lives, eh, Tony?"

"Yep. Do you guys want me to come with you, or would you rather I stay here?" Tony asked, surveying the surroundings of the house.

Lorne shrugged at Sally. "It's your call."

"Maybe it would be better if you stayed here, Tony."

Lorne and Sally walked across the deep gravelled drive, their heels sinking into the stones. "When we introduce ourselves, I think it would be wise just to give our ranks and leave out the part about what division we belong to," Lorne whispered as they stopped outside the front door.

"Any reason?"

"We're not deceiving anyone, just being economical with the truth. What's the harm in that?"

Sally shook her head and grinned. "Same old Lorne. Never give up anything without there being a good reason to."

Lorne nodded in agreement. "Cards and chest come to mind."

Sally rang the bell.

It was opened briskly by a blonde woman with blushing, mascara-stained cheeks. She looked disappointed when she saw Lorne and Sally waiting on the doorstep. "Yes?" she asked sharply.

"Lucy Timcott?" Sally asked as both she and Lorne flashed their warrant cards. "DI Sally Parker and DI Lorne Warner."

"That's right." She gasped, and her hand clutched the edges of her lace-trimmed cardigan at her chest. "Police? Does this mean that you've found my husband?" She looked beyond Lorne and Sally at the car. "Is that him?" her voice notched up a few octaves in expectation when she saw Tony's outline.

"No, I'm sorry. Perhaps it would be better if we discussed this inside," Lorne suggested.

The woman took a few steps back, then she led the way through the double-height entrance hall displaying stripped-oak beams on every available surface. Lorne considered the beautifully renovated barn conversion with interest and a fair amount of envy. It had always been her goal to reinstate the charm into a building as desirable as this. She would have fulfilled that ambition, too, if she had ignored her calling to return to the force, years ago. *I had my chance. Maybe once retirement hits, Tony and I can take up the challenge of renovating such a stunning place. Yeah, and there's a pig passing overhead now.*

"You have a very beautiful home," Lorne stated, her tone full of admiration.

The woman shrugged. No eager smile to agree, nothing. Instead, she opened the twin glass doors into the living room. When Sally and Lorne entered the room, Lorne was surprised to find a well-groomed woman in her sixties studying them.

In a trembling voice, Lucy announced, "Mum, it's the police."

"Ladies. I hope you're bringing us good news. My daughter, we've both, been worried sick about Ryan."

"Sorry, I didn't catch your name?" Lorne asked.

The woman's smoky-coloured made-up eyes turned Lorne's way and seemed to penetrate into her very soul. If the glare had come from a male, Lorne would have felt the need to shudder. Instead she found the glower emanating from this woman as a challenge. The woman left the heat of the open fire and walked towards them, her elegant ring-filled fingers extended, ready to shake hands. "It's a pleasure to meet you. I'm Lucy's mother, Claire Knight."

Sally was the first to shake hands with the woman. "DI Sally Parker. This is my colleague, DI Lorne Warner."

The woman smiled as she daintily shook hands with Lorne. She hated it when people didn't shake hands properly; she much preferred a firm handshake, even from women. Her father had always told her that a person can learn a lot from someone's handshake. The only thing Lorne picked up from Claire Knight was her sense of breeding. It was obvious from the woman's attire and the way she held her head that she'd enjoyed the high life from a very young age. That kind of demeanour could never be taught. "It's a pleasure to meet you, ladies. I don't think I've ever dealt with female officers of the law before."

What am I supposed to take from that? That you've had plenty of involvement with the police over the years? Or am I misreading your message?

"It used to be a male-orientated career years ago; not so much now. We're fighting back, shall we say." Lorne smiled tautly at the woman. "Would you mind if we sit down?"

"No, please do. Excuse my lack of manners," Lucy mumbled, inviting them all to take a seat.

Everyone sat except for Claire, who resumed her place in front of the fire, blocking the heat from penetrating the room. Lorne held back and let Sally conduct the conversation. Lorne's gaze flicked between mother and daughter as Sally issued the news regarding the victim.

The second Sally said 'your husband's body,' Lucy broke down and sobbed like any adoring wife would after finding out her husband had passed away. However, as Claire studied her daughter, Lorne noticed a coldness seep into the woman's eyes. She would even have gone as far as to describe it as hatred emanating from the woman's chestnut-coloured eyes. Admittedly, it only appeared for a split second, but Lorne had spotted it nevertheless. Then her hand rose to her cheek, and she made a small whimpering sound. The whole bizarre display stuck in Lorne's throat. Nothing about Claire's reaction seemed genuine.

As if sensing Lorne's eyes upon her, Claire rushed to her daughter's side to comfort her. "Darling, how awful. We'll ensure he's never forgotten."

'We'll ensure he's never forgotten'? Is that really the first thing a mother can come up with to console her daughter? Lorne had delivered the shocking news of a husband's demise dozens of times during her career. Never once had she stumbled across a situation as awkward as this.

Lorne glanced sideways at Sally, who, judging by her expression. Didn't think anything out of the ordinary was afoot. Lorne's disappointment intensified, and she hoped it wouldn't cause a rift between Sally and herself once they'd left the premises.

"Where?" Lucy managed to say before her throat clogged up with yet another sob.

"On his boat. We're under the impression that the vessel exploded in a bay off the Kent coast, sometime Sunday afternoon."

Lucy turned to look at her mother, who was kneeling at her side. "The Kent coast? What was he doing there?"

Sally extracted her notebook and began taking notes. Lorne did the same.

"Where did you think your husband was on Sunday, Lucy?" Sally asked.

"I knew he'd taken the boat out. I just wasn't aware of how far he'd gone."

Claire patted her daughter's hand and rose to her feet to stand alongside her daughter's chair. "You know what men are like. Keen to show off to their pals when they have a new toy, Inspector."

"I do," Sally agreed. "So, he left here at what time on Sunday?"

Lucy was silent for a few seconds as she contemplated her answer. Had the lengthy hesitation come from the mother, Lorne's suspicions would have multiplied. However, she didn't get the impression that Lucy was doing anything but trying to recall the actual time.

"It was around ten, I suppose. Yes, I had just started to prepare the Sunday roast."

"Ah, so from that, I take it you expected him to return within a few hours?" Sally asked, noting down the reply.

"Yes, we always eat around two. That would have given him enough time to show off to his friends and return home."

"Any friends in particular, Lucy? It might be an idea if we had a chat with them after we leave here."

Lucy shook her head. "My mind is all over the place. I can't think of anyone who would be interested in his new acquisition."

"What about John, Terry, or Bob?" Claire offered before Sally could ask another question.

"No, Mum, their families come first on a Sunday. I really can't see them being interested."

"Well, it was just a thought," Claire replied in a huff.

Lucy looked up at her mother as if she'd offended her. "I'm sorry, Mum. I know you're only trying to help, but I think I know my husband and his friends better than you do."

Claire took a few paces to her left, picked up a gold lighter, tapped a cigarette out of a packet, and proceeded to light it. Lorne's gaze flicked back to Lucy, who seemed annoyed by her mother's actions, although she remained quiet. Lorne sensed a certain amount of angst drifting between the mother and daughter. She'd never witnessed such behaviour in similar circumstances before. It was intriguing and uncomfortable at the same time. *Don't all mothers set out to support their daughters after devastating news of a family member's death?* Had the awkward conversation been taking place on her patch, Lorne might have tackled the mother about her attitude. Instead, she bit her tongue and watched the proceedings with mounting curiosity. She jotted down a few notes referencing her general thoughts about the strain in the relationship between the two women.

Thankfully, Sally stuck to her word about not mentioning the two women they suspected were involved in Ryan's death. "It would be helpful if you could supply us with a few names to contact, Lucy."

"And I'm expected to think of those names off the top of my head when all I can think about is my husband lying on a slab at a mortuary?"

"I understand it's asking a lot, but it would help us immensely to make a start on our investigation."

Her hand swept over her pale face. "I'm confused. What investigation? Oh, I see—you're investigating the explosion on behalf of the insurance company."

Sally exhaled a breath. "Not exactly. Although we will be getting in touch with them shortly. So if you can give us the details of the policy, that would also be a great help."

"Then what? I sense there's something you're keeping from me. I demand to know what it is," Lucy said as the colour rose in her cheeks.

Although Lorne's concerns were growing regarding Lucy's discomfort, her gaze continued to remain focused on Claire. The second her daughter's voice rose, Claire's eyes rolled up to the ceiling. Again, it lasted only for an instant before the deadpan expression settled on her face once more. But Lorne caught the mother's annoyance nevertheless. She made another note to tell Sally what she'd observed once they left.

"I'm struggling to see why your husband felt the need to keep his activities for the day a secret?" Sally asked.

"He *didn't*," Lucy retorted sharply. "He told me he was going out on his boat. There were no secrets between us. I can assure you of that, Inspector."

"And yet you had no idea of his intention to head south for the day. He clearly neglected, or avoided, informing you about his possible lengthy absence, because you didn't break your routine of preparing the Sunday lunch that you expected him to attend. Now can you understand my confusion, Lucy?"

The young woman took a few short breaths before she responded. "I'm sorry to fly off the handle. Yes, of course I understand your line of questioning and confusion. I'm afraid it won't alter my reply. Wait a minute, if Ryan died on the boat, are you telling me he was alone?"

Sally nodded. "That's exactly what I'm telling you, another reason for my confusion, considering you've just told us that he was heading out to show off his boat to friends. Something doesn't add up."

Lucy buried her head in her hands and started to cry. An uneasy silence descended over the room. Lorne eyed Claire to see if she would rush to her daughter's side again to comfort her—she didn't. Instead, Claire pulled heavily on her cigarette and simply stared at Lucy. Lorne sensed then that the woman lacked any kind of maternal instinct and that the initial signs of concern she had shown her daughter were likely for Lorne and Sally's benefit. Claire glanced Lorne's way and caught Lorne studying her. Any normal mother would have blushed, reconsidered her actions, and swept down to at least throw an arm around her daughter's shoulder. Not Claire Knight. Her eyes sparkled with a challenge. Lorne trawled her mind and realised she had encountered an equally uncomfortable reaction from only one person in her working life—from her all-time nemesis, the Unicorn. Thankfully, Lorne suppressed the temptation to shudder. The last thing she wanted to do was to let on that this woman had a strange effect on her. She held Claire's stare for a moment or two longer until the other woman's gaze returned to her daughter.

"Come now, Lucy, breaking down every five minutes isn't going to bring Ryan back. The detectives have work to do. Just tell them what they need to know and let them get on with their investigation."

Glaring at her mother, Lucy slowly lowered her hands and took a tissue from her sleeve to wipe the tears from her face. Lorne sensed Lucy was chewing large lumps out of her tongue rather than have a screaming fit at her mother in front of them.

Sally cleared her throat and smiled at Lucy. "There's no rush. We'd much rather stay here with you to ensure you're okay before chasing up other lines of enquiries."

Claire's eyebrow rose for a split second. Lorne wondered what that indicated. *Do you know more about your son-in-law's death than you're willing to let on about, Claire Knight? If we pushed you hard enough, would the cracks begin to show? Maybe you're one of the women we're trying to track down.*

"Other lines of enquiry?" Lucy asked after she'd mulled over the statement for a few seconds.

"Yes. Until we have something concrete to hand, I think it would be best if I didn't say anything further about that."

"Why? Because you're lying?" Claire challenged, surprising Lorne with the amount of venom resonating in her accusation.

Sally shrugged calmly. "Not at all. We have a few witness statements that we need to look into over the next few days. Our main aim was to visit Lucy as soon as her husband's identity had been verified. That's the usual sequence of events in this type of enquiry."

"Accidents happen all the time on boats. Do you always get involved in such crimes?" Claire asked.

"Sometimes. It depends if these 'accidents' turn out to be something far more sinister instead," Sally replied.

Lorne mentally high-fived Sally for handling the woman's obnoxious behaviour the way she would have. *Yep, I can see we're going to have a lot of fun tackling this case together, Sally. It's going to be like old times.*

Mother and daughter exchanged confused looks. "So, does that mean you're intending to treat this investigation as something other than an accident, Inspector?" Claire demanded.

"As I've already told you, Mrs. Knight, our investigation has only just commenced. Very rarely do these types of cases get solved with a click of the fingers. There will be witness statements to corroborate, DNA evidence to sift through… the list really is endless. That's why it's essential that we get the investigation off to a good start. I have to ask, Lucy, can you think of anyone who would wish to harm your husband?"

Lucy's forehead wrinkled. "No, not in the least. You're not making sense. Are you saying that you think my husband has been murdered?"

Claire left her position beside the fire and walked over to the patio doors overlooking the rear garden.

Lorne swivelled in her chair to keep an eye on the mother.

Claire lit up yet another cigarette and tutted. "Looks like developing that new barbecue area will need to be put on hold for now, Lucy."

Lorne fought hard to prevent her mouth from dropping open. She turned to look at Lucy.

The poor woman looked stunned by her mother's incomprehensible observation. "Mother! How could you think of such a thing at a time like this?"

"Life goes on, cherub. I'm just trying to be practical, as always. Sorry, ignore me. You usually do anyway," she replied tersely, her gaze never leaving the landscaped gardens.

Sally repeated the question, "Sorry, did your husband have any enemies?"

Lucy heaved out a quivering breath. "No, not that I can think of. Please, can this wait a few days? I haven't come to terms with my loss as yet, and you're asking me to come up with details that I really can't do right now."

"I understand. I'll leave you my card. If a name suddenly comes to mind, will you ring me, immediately? Day or night. The quicker we can get on the trail of a possible candidate, the better."

Lucy accepted the card. "I promise. At the moment, my mind is just a blur. I don't know what I'm going to do without my husband. I need time to grieve before I can even contemplate helping you with your investigation. Please don't think I'm being awkward."

Sally smiled. "I don't. One last question before we go." She turned to address the mother. "Mrs. Knight, do you live here?"

The woman turned to face the rest of them and laughed, then she puffed on her cigarette. "Oh no, I couldn't live out in a dingy backwater like this. No offence, Lucy, but we've had this conversation many times over the years."

Sally inclined her head. "I see. May I ask why you're here if you are so anti-Norfolk?"

"I would have thought that was obvious, Inspector—to support my daughter. Her husband *was* missing!" she added sarcastically.

"And where do you usually reside, Mrs. Knight?" Sally asked with the tautest of smiles.

"The bright lights of London. There's no better city in this world and nowhere else I'd prefer to call home."

"Ah, my neck of the woods," Lorne told the woman.

"I thought I caught a London accent when you spoke. Are you on some kind of exchange?"

"No. This case will be a jointly run investigation, covering the two counties. Look at it this way: you get two reputable police forces and two indomitable inspectors working the case. We'll get the answers we seek in half the time. That's our aim anyway."

"As long as you don't get in each other's way and end up looking like that inept mob the Keystone Cops." Claire laughed at her own joke, even if no one else in the room did.

Lucy tutted, her annoyance clear.

"No fear of that, Mrs. Knight. Lorne and I have both won numerous accolades for our expertise over the years. We don't stop until we have the criminals put behind bars where they belong, even if that means putting our own lives in harm's way."

Claire raised an eyebrow. "That's very reassuring. I hope you don't end up living to regret making that fine speech, Inspector."

"We won't. I can assure you of that."

Sally and Lorne rose from their chairs at the same time. Lucy also stood and showed them to the front door. Sally shook Lucy's hand. "Don't forget, ring me day or night with any concerns or if a name comes to mind. I'm sorry for your loss."

"Thank you. You've both been very kind." Lucy looked over her shoulder then added, "You'll have to excuse my mother. She's not the easiest of people to get along with. She's stubborn and prefers to be in control of everything she does. This happening has meant that she is out of her comfort zone."

Lorne shook Lucy's hand. "Maybe it would be better if she left you alone to grieve in that case."

"I think you might be right, Inspector. I'll make sure she leaves by the end of today. My nerves are in tatters now. Another few hours of her demeaning put-me-downs will serve neither of us well in the long run. Please, don't let her lukewarm attitude hinder your willingness to conduct your investigation."

Sally smiled. "No need to worry about that, Lucy. It's already forgotten. Take care. We'll be in touch again soon."

Tony was outside the car, enjoying the odd ray of sun as it peeped through the clouds. "How did it go?"

Lorne and Sally looked at each other and shrugged. Lorne opened the passenger door of the car. "Hard to say really. One thing I'm certain about though is that the mother, Claire Knight, has put herself firmly on my radar. I'm going to have fun delving into her background to see what she's been up to over the years. I get the impression she doesn't care much for other women or female police officers."

"I think you've hit the nail on the head there, Lorne," Sally replied, jumping behind the steering wheel.

"Perhaps we missed a trick."

Sally turned in Lorne's direction as she started the car. "What about?"

"Maybe we should have told them about the two women, if only to gauge their reaction."

Sally put her foot down and drove a fair distance from the house before she replied. "Let's look at it as a piece of evidence we can use in our favour to tease some more information out of them during our next visit."

"Sounds good to me," Lorne replied, nodding thoughtfully.

CHAPTER NINE

The instant Lucy left the room with the policewomen, Claire sprang into action. She fished her mobile phone out of her handbag and prodded angrily at the number one on her keypad. The call was answered after the second ring.

"Hello, Mother. How's Lucy holding up?"

"Cut the crap, Teagan. Your sickly sweet disposition might work on the others, but I see through that bloody façade, girl."

"I don't know what you mean, Mother. All I did was enquire about my sister's good health. Have I done something wrong?"

Claire inhaled a sharp breath, letting her daughter know how annoyed she was at being given the run-around. "You did this! Your twisted way of dealing with things has brought all this trouble to our door. Now, because of your misguided judgement, we've got not one, but two, bloody police areas on our backs. Well, what do you have to say for yourself?"

"So what? Let them investigate the crime. They'll come up blank. We covered our tracks properly, Mother, just like you instilled in us from a young age."

"I doubt that. Why did you have to kill him?"

"Because…"

"I don't have time to listen to your bloody ludicrous excuses. I have to figure out a way to get us out of this mess, and quickly. Are you aware that you left a trail of witnesses?"

"Nope, none as far as we could see. The coppers are just trying to scare you. They've got nothing to prove that we were ever on that boat," Teagan suggested arrogantly.

Claire knew that her daughter had approached things like a downhill skier and come up short before the end of the slope. "We'll see about that. These women have what appears to be a steely determination about them. I wouldn't go thinking you've got away with anything just yet, my girl. It will serve you right if you get caught—you shouldn't have challenged me. Will you never learn?"

"You're right about one thing, Mother. In your eyes, I'll never do anything right. However, I have learnt something over the years, while you've been rubbing your hands at my lack of progression."

"What the hell are you talking about, girl?"

"I've learnt to always have a card up my sleeve. In my case, that just happens to be an ace."

"I repeat, what the hell are you talking about, Teagan?"

"You'll find out soon enough. Just remember one thing, Mother dearest: over the years you've moulded me to be just like you. What you hadn't bargained on, is me being smarter and more determined than you've ever been."

Claire was seething at the disrespect Teagan was showing, but she had no intention of revealing how much her daughter's attitude was getting to her. "What are you planning, Teagan? I demand to know!"

"You'll discover that when everyone else finds out."

Claire angrily disconnected the call just as Lucy entered the room.

"Mother? Is everything all right?" Lucy asked, looking perplexed.

Claire pulled her shoulders back and stood erect. "Nothing for you to worry about. It's just your sister playing silly buggers again. Now the police have gone, I suppose we should begin to organise Ryan's funeral, then there's the life insurance cover to sort out. Do you intend to remain living out here, or are you going to move back to London to be with the rest of your family?"

Lucy's eyes fluttered shut, and when she opened them again, bulging tears dripped onto her cheeks. "I can't think about that kind of thing at the moment, Mum. I need to grieve. I loved Ryan. He was my soulmate. The one man who made me *feel* whole, like a real woman. Please allow me to grieve before insisting I deal with all the damned paperwork associated with someone's death."

Claire walked over to the patio doors again and muttered, "Do what you have to do, child." *Falling out with Teagan is as much as I can take for one day.*

CHAPTER TEN

During the return journey to the station, Lorne and Sally agreed that the investigation would take two routes. Since Claire had shown her hand, Lorne urgently wanted to dig into the woman's past. Most of all, she was intrigued to find out what kind of involvement she'd had with the police over the years. Lorne contacted Katy and relayed the information they'd gathered, which was minimal, regarding the woman's name and where she lived. She instructed Katy to carry out thorough background checks on Knight and the rest of the family residing in London.

This left Sally and her team free to investigate Lucy Timcott and Ryan's friends and colleagues.

Tony looked on in admiration as the team went about their tasks.

Lorne pulled up a chair and sat alongside him. "Are you regretting coming up here, Tony? You're looking a little lost."

"Of course not. I must admit I'm feeling a little left out. Perhaps if you gave me a job to do, I might feel more included in the case."

Lorne pecked him on the cheek. "I have to admit, I'm feeling a tad like that myself. What do you suggest we do about that?"

Tony shrugged. "I know what I'd prefer to be doing right now." He winked and reached over to squeeze her thigh.

Lorne's cheeks heated up. "Control yourself, Mr. Warner."

"Killjoy! Seriously, I need something to occupy me, Lorne. Sitting here, twiddling my fingers like this, is going to drive me nuts."

"I appreciate that, hon. Bear with me. I'll have a word with Sally, see what we can come up with." Lorne crossed the room and stopped a few feet behind Sally, waiting for her to finish her phone conversation. "Hi," Lorne said when she'd hung up.

Sally's hand covered her breasts. "Bloody hell, Lorne." She thumped at her chest. "I need to get my heart pumping again. Have you discovered anything?"

"Sorry. Only that my husband is bored. I couldn't help overhearing your conversation. Umm... who exactly were you making a date with?"

Sally rolled her eyes up to the ceiling. "And that concerns you *how*?" she asked, grinning like the Cheshire cat.

"Sounded like you know the person well, as if you work with them in some way. Another copper perhaps?"

Sally perched on the desk behind her and crossed her arms. "Nope. Nice try. My lips are sealed on this one. Why is Tony bored? Should I have given him a task, too?"

"You know he's a PI, right?"

"Crap, that fact had momentarily slipped my mind. Hey, don't have a go at me. You're aware of how painstakingly slow an investigation is until it gets going."

"Yeah, I completely understand. He just hates being inside. It doesn't take long before it sends him stir-crazy."

"What about if I let him work alongside Jack? An ex-military man and an ex-MI6 agent—now that should prove to be interesting."

"It depends what Jack is doing."

"The same as the rest of us, looking into the backgrounds of Lucy and Ryan and getting exceedingly frustrated with the results."

Lorne beckoned for Tony to join them. "Sally suggested you teaming up with her partner, Jack. Are you up for that?"

A small smile broke out on his face. "Sounds good to me."

Lorne's mobile rang as Sally led Tony towards her partner's desk. "Hi, Katy. I hope you're having more success than we are right now?"

"Are you sitting down?"

Lorne plopped into the nearest chair and extracted her notebook from her jacket pocket. She flipped it open to a blank page. "I am now. What do you have?"

"The answer to that is one word: shitloads. We're still sifting through it now, but I can give you a rundown on the highlights, if you like?"

"Bugger, maybe I made the wrong call in coming up here."

"I'm not saying a word on that front. Right, are you ready for this?"

"Hit me with it. You're going to tell me this woman has got a rap sheet as long as the Thames, aren't you?"

Katy laughed. "That might be a slight exaggeration on your part. The problem is, there are plenty of incidents noted down, but she's never been actually charged with anything."

"That sounds crazy. Why?"

"Not enough evidence," Katy confirmed.

"What kind of cases are we dealing with, Katy?"

"How about this for starters? She's been widowed twice."

Lorne paused. "I'm not with you. How can she be held accountable there?"

"Both of her husbands' deaths were suspicious, yet the cases were never closed."

"Never *closed*? You're right—that is strange. Want to share the details?"

Katy spent the next five minutes running through the limited facts she had for both cases. "Whoa! Either she's one hell of an unlucky woman, or she's a canny bitch who recognises an opening when she sees it to get rid of a loved one without raising suspicions."

"Yep, that's my assumption, too."

"Is she married now?"

"According to the records, she's recently divorced."

"At least this one escaped with his life. Any reports on his life being put in jeopardy?"

"I searched for that, and no, nothing along those lines has come to our attention so far."

"She strikes me as an evil bitch. The type who makes your skin prickle when you shake hands with them." Lorne lowered her voice and continued, "I really didn't want to cause a fuss as Sally led the questioning while I observed, but, boy, I couldn't take my eyes off her. She reminds me of one of those old-time Hollywood actresses, if you know what I mean? Seemed almost blasé about Ryan's death, as if she was keen for Lucy to forget about him and move on to the next one."

"Given what we've discovered about her past this morning, I'm not surprised to hear that. Is she staying up there for a few days?"

"Touchy subject. I think Lucy is going to try and get rid of her. She regarded her daughter's home as being set out in the backwaters. Yet the place was stunning. It comes with its own mooring, too."

"Could it be a case of the mother envying her daughter's possessions?"

Lorne shook her head and tapped her pen on the desk as she pondered. "I didn't really get that impression, Katy. She's definitely a complex character, one that we need to keep an eye on when she returns home. When that will be, I haven't got the foggiest."

"Well, I'll keep digging at this end. I just thought you'd prefer to know that information ASAP."

"Brilliant work. I think you've come up with more than we've managed to obtain at this end so far. Oh, by the way, when we asked

Lucy where she thought her husband was on the day of his death, she told us that he'd taken delivery of the new boat and was out showing it off to friends. Ryan told her that he was going out with friends, never even mentioned his intention of travelling to Kent. The question is, why?"

"That is strange. Maybe it was a cover-up just to have an orgy with the two women, you know, to *christen* his new craft. Who knows what crazy ideas go through these men's heads when they have a new toy to show off, especially an expensive one like that?"

"Good point. This case is already starting to make us question the individual family members' motives. Something tells me that this is just the beginning in that respect. Keep digging, Katy. Don't forget the other family members, too."

"I won't. If I find anything significant, I'll call you straight away. Enjoy your visit out there in the backwaters of civilisation." Katy was still laughing when she disconnected the call.

Sally approached Lorne, looking puzzled. "Everything all right?"

"Depends how you define 'all right.' That was my partner. She's come up with some interesting facts about Claire Knight."

"Are you willing to share those facts with me at this point, or do I need to use the thumbscrews I have tucked away in my drawer?" Sally joked.

Lorne shook her head to dislodge the image her friend's words had conjured up in her mind. "Is that how police work is carried out up here in the backwaters?"

"You've clearly been listening to Mrs. Knight too much." They both laughed, then Lorne revealed what Katy had divulged moments earlier. "Okay, well that puts a different slant on things. Both of her husbands' deaths were suspicious, and here we are looking at yet another suspicious death of another husband, albeit her daughter's. There's too much information there for it to be coincidence, wouldn't you say?"

"My thinking exactly. What if the mother was one of those women aboard Ryan's boat? Is that even feasible?" Lorne asked pensively.

"It's feasible all right. Whether Knight seems the type of woman to dress up like a dog's dinner is another question entirely."

"Oops… yes, I forgot that part." Lorne chuckled. "Let's not rule the possibility out just yet. I get the distinct impression that Knight is the type of woman who doesn't suffer fools gladly, and when she has her mind set on something, nothing—and I mean nothing—will get in her way of achieving it."

"So, where do we go from here?"

"We keep digging. Anything suspicious we find out about this family at this point needs to be put under the microscope. I'm going to ask Katy to send over the details of Knight's husbands' deaths, see if I can find anything that the investigating officers missed."

"Good idea. Did Katy mention what kind of business they were in by any chance?"

Lorne shook her head. "No, I'll be sure to ask when I ring her. Any luck on tracking down some of Ryan's friends? What about his place of work? Maybe he had a partner who he confided in?"

"I'll get the boys, Jack and Tony on that now." Sally cringed. "I've just remembered I need to fill my chief in. If he walks in and sees you and Tony here, he'll have a cardiac arrest."

"Seriously? Does he have a dodgy ticker?" Lorne queried.

"Not that I'm aware of. Maybe I used the wrong phraseology. I'll be right back."

The instant Sally left the incident room, Lorne called Katy back and requested the files be sent to Jack's e-mail address. Jack printed out the files, and Lorne began searching through the papers just as a disgruntled Sally re-joined the team.

"I take it the chief wasn't that enamoured with our intrusion?" Lorne asked.

Sally's lips twisted. "He's rarely happy anyway, so I tend not to take much notice most of the time. I emphasised that you were the lead investigator and that we were just lending a hand, but if any arrests were made, both forces would take the credit. I hope that was okay?"

Lorne tutted and punched her friend lightly on the arm. "Of course, that makes perfect sense to me. Did you put his mind at ease and tell him that we only intended to stay around here for a few days?"

"No, it slipped my mind. Actually, I was too busy being amused by the amount of steam escaping from his ears."

"I guess I'm lucky in that respect. Sean Roberts is a pretty easy-going chief. When he steps out of line, all I have to do is offer him my resignation. He reconsiders his actions immediately."

"She isn't joking about that, either," Tony called out.

CHAPTER ELEVEN

Teagan paced the room, livid about what her mother had said over the phone. She turned to her sister. "I need to know you're with me on this, Helen."

"I've told you I am, but after what happened to Ryan, it's going to cost you."

Teagan sighed. "All right. How much are we talking about? Bearing in mind that it'll be mostly me who is going to be taking all the bloody risks and feeling Mother's wrath, to boot."

"Fifty grand."

Teagan stopped in front of her sister. Eyes bulging, she asked, "What? Are you fucking crazy?"

"No, I'm dead bloody serious. You have no idea the amount of debt Frank left me in when he ran off a few months back."

"Jesus, woman, when are you going to learn to keep your legs shut? When are you going to damn *learn*, full stop? These men are crafty. They all set out to do one thing, end up in your bed. The minute they achieve that, they can't wait to get away from you."

Helen sneered at her. "It's great to know I can count on you to give my dwindling self-esteem a boost."

"It's the truth, whether you wish to accept it or not. You flash your cash and your tits to snare these men. Once the novelty has worn off with them, they flee from your bed as if it's in flames."

"I can't help it if I fall for the wrong type of men."

"Once, I can accept. But half a dozen times, Helen? When's it going to end? Mother instilled into us at very young age how to manipulate men for our own benefits. Have you forgotten the tricks she taught you?" Her sister's mouth dropped open. Teagan was on a roll and decided to get a few more things off her chest while she had her younger sister's attention. "How do you get into debt for fifty grand while conforming to Mother's teachings? Does she know about the debt?"

Helen fell into the chair and leaned her head back to look up at the ceiling. "I messed up. Got charmed by the wrong guy, and no, mother hasn't got a clue about the debt." Helen suddenly sat forward in the chair and anxiously added, "She'd string me up if she knew about that. You won't tell her, will you?"

"I give up. First you tap me up for fifty grand, and then you expect me to keep shtum about it if Mother's suspicions become raised."

"If that sort of dosh is on the table, then I'm up for giving it a go," Olga, Teagan's youngest sister, said from the doorway.

"Do you mind? This is a private conversation," Teagan admonished swiftly.

Olga shrugged. "All right. I'll be sure to let it slip into the conversation the next time I speak to Mother." Olga turned to walk away.

"Wait! You win! The pair of you really do piss me off at times. You, Helen, with your calamitous taste in men, and you, Olga, with that repugnant drug habit of yours. May I ask what you intend doing with fifty grand, *if* such a sum was actually sitting on the table?"

Olga wiped a hand under her nostrils. Teagan convulsed at the thought of the outrageous amount of money her sister had snorted in the last few months. That route had never interested Teagan in the slightest, and she had a hard time dealing with her sister's out-of-control habit. The last thing she wanted was to give Olga the funds to fuel her habit even more.

"I'd use it to book myself into rehab," Olga said.

Teagan's eyes narrowed when her sister's gaze shifted quickly. "Are you for *real*?"

"I said so, didn't I? You think I enjoy living on the edge like this?" Olga shouted. "I despise it. But I'm in too deep, hooked, with nowhere to go. I need to seek professional help. This money would keep me at the facility until the withdrawal symptoms end. That's when the hard part begins. I can do this, with your help. What do I need to do in return?"

Teagan felt proud of her sister wanting to clean up her act. However she'd heard an addict's ability to lie increased tenfold the deeper the addiction grew. But the willingness to believe her sister wanting to better her life challenged that fact. "What do you think, Helen? Is our little sister ready to get in on the family act?"

"How the fuck should I know? Looks like you've got a decision to make, because we're both desperate for that money."

"Eenie, meenie… which of you two do I trust the most?" Teagan placed her thumb and forefinger on either side of her chin as she contemplated the answer.

"To do what?" Olga asked again.

Teagan smiled broadly. "To *kill*, Olga. Do you have the balls to do that?"

CHAPTER TWELVE

Lorne glanced up from her notes to find that it was almost six o'clock. Sally's team had started to drift home for the evening, and Sally looked ready to call it a day soon, too.

Tony sat on the corner of the desk she'd been allocated. "I could do with a beer. What's the plan? Are we going to book into a hotel room for the night?"

Lorne looked over her shoulder at her friend. "I think Sally's expecting us to stay at her house with her folks. Is that okay with you?"

"I guess it will have to be. Although, I'd much rather be holed up in a hotel room with my sexy wife. I'm willing to forgo my elicit wish if I have to."

"That's it, make me feel guilty."

"About what?" Sally asked, sneaking up behind Lorne.

"Marital dispute, a tiny one at that. What's the plan for tonight? Is there a nearby hotel or motel where we can rest our weary heads?"

Sally shook her head. "Nope, you're staying with us. No arguments. Mum and Dad will be disappointed if you don't. Mum's cooking one of her extra-special roast dinners for the occasion. You wouldn't want to miss out on that."

"Now I feel bad. I didn't want to cause your mum any trouble."

"Nonsense, you aren't. I suggested we go out for a meal, but she was adamant. She's looking forward to seeing you again, Lorne. I just hope Tony won't be too bored."

"You women worry too much. As long as the beer or wine is flowing, we men are very appreciative of a good meal and lively chatter."

"That's settled, then. After dinner, you can keep my parents entertained regaling them with your wondrous MI6 stories, Tony, while Lorne and I take Dex for a walk down by the river." Sally winked at Lorne then added, "That way I get out of the washing-up duties."

Lorne snorted. "Bit harsh when your mum has gone to so much trouble cooking a special dinner."

Sally shrugged. "I know, shit happens."

Lorne had a feeling her friend was teasing her and that nothing could be farther from the truth. She was looking forward to meeting Sally's parents, and seeing the smile break out on Tony's face made her think he was more than happy to chat away endlessly to Sally's parents.

As soon as the trio entered the house, Dex, a young golden Labrador, ran up to Sally and greeted her enthusiastically. He tried his hardest to communicate with his master and share his affection equally between the three of them

"He's adorable. Charlie would fall head over heels in love with him. If ever you get bored with him, let me know, and I'll gladly take him off your hands," Lorne ruffled the dog's head.

Sally pulled Dex into her arms and cupped her hands over his ears. "Don't listen to her, Dex. We'd never get bored of you, sweetums."

The dog's moaning increased in pitch and decibels.

"All right, enough is enough. We don't want you getting overexcited. We want a peaceful evening, and then we'll go for a long walk later, weather permitting of course." She looked up at Lorne. "Remind me to take the torch with us. It'll be dark along by the river."

"Hello there." Chris, Sally's father, greeted them with a huge smile. He hugged Lorne and shook hands with Tony. "Welcome to our humble home. It's by no means a palace, but it makes us happy living here."

"Seems like a nice neighbourhood," Tony said.

Sally and her father glanced at each other and laughed. "It is now," Sally admitted. "It's a long story. I'll tell you the tale over dinner."

"Sounds intriguing. I'm dying to see your mum," Lorne said as they made their way down the hall and into the kitchen.

Janine seemed flustered as she darted around the kitchen. Sally grabbed her mother's shoulders, forcing her to stop for a few minutes. "Lorne, how wonderful to see you again after all this time. You haven't changed a bit."

Lorne hugged Janine. "I have to repay the compliment, Janine. You look stunning, if a little flustered. Can I lend a hand with anything? No good asking my husband; he only deals with charred offerings."

"Charming… don't listen to her, Janine. I taught her everything she knows in the kitchen."

Lorne spun around and swiped his arm. "Why, you cheeky little…"

"Now, now children, we don't want any domestic wrangles this evening," Chris warned playfully. "I'm going to break open a couple of bottles of red, if that's agreeable to everyone."

"Not on our account, I hope. We should have dropped by the off-licence on our way home. Sorry. Not very thoughtful of me, given your kindness," Lorne replied sheepishly.

"We don't do self-recrimination in this house, Lorne. You're our guests," Chris said, opening the cupboard and reaching for the large wine glasses.

Over dinner, the conversation was jovial until Janine asked, "Do your parents live in London, Lorne?"

Lorne picked up her glass, sat back in her chair, and smiled. "Unfortunately, neither of them are with us now. Mum passed away from cancer about fifteen years ago, and Dad died from a heart attack after recovering from meningitis nearly five years ago. The galling part is we all thought he was on the mend." Lorne sighed heavily. "I've always blamed myself for his demise."

Tony grabbed one of her hands and kissed the back of it. "Nonsense, Lorne. When it's time for someone special to leave us, that's when they slip away, often when we're least expecting it."

"Tony's right, love. Why do you blame yourself?" Janine asked quietly, gathering Sally's hand in her own and squeezing it tightly enough to make her daughter wince.

"My partner and I messed up an investigation and ended up getting ourselves abducted by slave traders. I still cringe when I think of what would have happened if…" She leaned over and kissed Tony on the cheek. "If my real-life hero hadn't come to our rescue."

"How wonderful, but how did that affect your father's health?" Janine asked before the realisation struck her. She waved the notion away. "Ignore me. I can be a little dumb at times. So the stress of the situation caused your father to have a heart attack, is that right?"

"It didn't help matters. Although I suspect the relief of knowing Katy and I were both safe was more of a contributing factor to his sudden departure." Lorne's gaze drifted down to the table. "I was so excited to see him I rushed in the back door of the house, only to find him slumped over the kitchen table." She wiped a tear on the back of her hand. "He's still around us, though. I have a very dear psychic friend who assures me that both dad and Pete, my first partner on the job, are watching over me." Lorne spotted the puzzlement cross her friend's face. "We've already had this conversation, haven't we, Sally?"

Sally chewed her lip. "It's not really for me, Lorne, not that I've had any real dealings with psychics."

"Don't knock it until you try it. That's what my old dad used to say. Katy felt the same way, too, until recently."

"What made her change her mind?" Janine asked. "By the way, I'm a believer."

Sally looked sharply in her mother's direction. "Really, Mum? You've never told me that."

"I'm allowed to have secrets, dear." Janine winked at her daughter.

"Carol, my psychic friend, who also lends a hand at the rescue centre, helped us to solve a case." Tony chuckled, making Lorne correct herself. "All right, let me rephrase that. A victim who sadly lost her life was instrumental in guiding Carol to where her murder took place, which ultimately led Katy and me to arrest the murder suspect. I doubt he would ever have been discovered if it hadn't been for Carol and Noelle's input. Don't ever rule out using a psychic, Sally. Hey, my partner, Pete, was the biggest sceptic around. I have a feeling he's regretting his harsh words to Carol now, because he spends most of his time watching over me and is prone to popping up unexpectedly when I'm in need of assistance." Lorne smiled as his chubby face entered her mind.

"It sounds like you've always been surrounded by good people, Lorne," Janine suggested.

"I've never really thought about it that way, Janine." She winked at Tony. "And he's the best husband around. There's no doubting that fact."

Janine raised her husband's hand. "I think I can challenge you on that one, dear."

Out of the corner of her eye, Lorne noticed Sally's head drop. She placed a finger under Sally's chin, forcing her to meet her gaze. "You'll find someone special of your own soon enough. Promise me you won't let your disastrous marriage to Darryl put you off tying the knot in the future. There truly are some decent guys around. Tony and your dad are living proof of that, hon. Don't forget, my marriage to Tom was a pretty shambolic affair."

Sally smiled at Lorne. "I know. You understand how hard it is to trust when you've suffered gravely at the hands of a partner, don't you?"

"I do. When the right time presents itself, you'll understand what I mean." Lorne added mischievously, "If it hasn't already, that is."

Sally's cheeks turned scarlet, and she swiftly exchanged awkward glances with her parents.

"Oh, yes, what's all this, then?" her mother teased.

Acting innocent, Lorne bit her lip. "Sorry, have I spoken out of turn?"

Sally pointed at her. "I'll pay you back for that."

"Are you holding out on us, Sally Parker?" Janine prompted.

"Time to go for that walk, Lorne. Tony, do you want to join us, or would you rather entertain my parents with your spy stories?" Sally rose from the table, avoiding eye contact with her mother, ignoring her intrusive question.

"Would you mind if I give it a miss, Sally? My leg is a little sore."

Lorne patted her husband on the thigh, grateful he'd opted to remain at the house, giving her the opportunity to catch up with her friend.

Janine pounced swiftly. "What's wrong with your leg, Tony?"

Lorne cringed and closed her eyes when she saw Tony's hands dip under the table. *Bloody hell, here comes the damn party trick!* Upon hearing Janine and Sally gasp, she opened her eyes to see Tony holding his prosthetic limb and pointing at an area on the calf.

"I have a slight niggle here. It'll be fine later. Don't worry."

Lorne was the first person to burst into laughter, followed by Tony and Chris. Eventually, Sally and Janine recovered from the shock to see the funny side of Tony's off-the-wall prank.

"Oh my, dare I ask how that occurred?" Janine asked, taking a large gulp of wine from her glass.

"Courtesy of the Taliban during a covert operation. It's no big deal, Janine, a little inconvenient at times when I get stuck in the mud in the paddock at home, nothing major."

Again, they all laughed.

Lorne tugged Sally's arm. "You mentioned something about a walk? I've heard this tale a thousand times over and lived through the hell of his recuperation for months; I don't need to hear or think about it again, hon."

Sensing where they were going, Dex excitedly ran to pick up his lead. Sally popped the torch in her pocket, and they set off. When they returned three quarters of an hour later, they found an open-mouthed Janine and Chris sitting at the table, enthralled by Tony's tales.

CHAPTER THIRTEEN

The following morning, after a relatively comfortable night, Lorne, Tony, and Sally set off for the station in their separate cars. As Tony drove, Lorne answered her mobile. "Hi, Katy. How's it going back at the ranch?"

"It's proving to be very interesting."

"Do tell. Maybe we should head back if things are hotting-up down there," Lorne replied. "I'm going to put you on speaker so Tony can hear, okay?"

"Sure and yes, I think you should return, if you consider things have dried up at that end. After I sent you the files of the old cases relating to Claire Knight, I started making enquiries into what's going on in the woman's life now."

"And? I can tell you're excited about something. Spill, partner."

"Although we can't interview her former husbands for obvious reasons, we can have a word with her most recent beau. She divorced Allan Watts earlier this year."

"Great work. Have you made contact with him yet?"

"No, that's the next step on my agenda. He lives in the heart of the city."

"Okay, what about the marital home? Did she buy him out, or did he give it to her as part of the divorce settlement?"

"I knew you would ask about that."

"Sorry to be so predictable. Once you've experienced a divorce, it's the little things that bother you the most."

"Well, I looked at the land registry, and although the house was once registered in his name, that all changed about a month before the divorce was finalised."

"Very interesting. I wonder what Knight brought to the party, in the way of possessions? Umm… also, why is she currently called Knight and not Watts? What made her drop his name so quickly?"

"I need to pay him a visit to ask those questions, and more."

"I think we should see if anything has surfaced at this end overnight. Then, if Sally doesn't mind, we should get on the road. We could be back in London around midday," Tony suggested, glancing at the clock on the dashboard.

"It would be great if you could conduct the questioning, Lorne."

She was aware how self-conscious Katy had become since her bump had started to develop. "You've got it. We'll ring when we're on our way. Take it easy, Katy. Just keep digging for dirt. By what I've read so far, I'm sure we're going to uncover a mountain of questionable activity we can hit this *lady* with, and I use the term loosely. Externally, she might exude ladylike qualities, but I bet the more we dig up on her, that idea will be tossed aside pretty damn quickly."

"All right. One question before you go, if I may? What's your interpretation of the daughter, Lucy?"

"She seems genuine enough. Who can tell at this early stage? I sensed a certain amount of animosity between the mother and daughter. It's unclear what that was about. We'll bear her in mind as the investigation progresses. Sally's going to question Ryan's friends today, I believe. Maybe they'll be able to fill in the gaps on that front."

"Rightio, the team is busy delving into the other family members' pasts now. We're still no further forward with identifying these two mysterious women at this point."

"Don't fret about that for now. Maybe I should get in touch with Gemma at the TV station again and ask her to run an update story. Have we got the artist impressions back on the witnesses yet?"

"Yes. Want me to get in touch with her?"

"Great idea. If nothing else, the fact that these women's pictures are paraded on TV might spook them into making a major slipup."

"We can live in hope on that one. If the artist's impressions are any good. Be in touch soon." Katy hung up.

"Very interesting, eh?" Lorne rested her head back against the cushioned headrest.

"Like you say, if we keep the pressure on, someone will mess up sooner or later. They have to."

They followed Sally into the station car park. "You're lucky to live in such a beautiful area, Sally. What a peaceful drive into work that was compared to the mass traffic jams I have to contend with every day, driving into London."

"It has its moments, Lorne, especially when there are major roadworks. Drivers' brains turn to mush when their autopilot journey is disrupted."

"My partner just called. Looks like things are coming together a little down there."

"So you're going back?"

"Would you mind?"

Sally shrugged. "Not at all. It makes perfect sense, considering where the crime occurred. We'll keep digging and asking questions at this end and keep you up to date if anything shows up. I'm going to be questioning Ryan's friends today. That's the aim anyway. Are you going to get on the road now? You should miss the main crush on the A11 at this time of the morning."

"That's what we were thinking. I told Katy we'd be back just before lunch."

"Do you want to see if we've had any developments overnight first?"

Lorne smiled. "You read my mind. Maybe we could grab a quick coffee with you then take off."

The three of them entered the station only to be disappointed by the news that nothing new concerning the case had appeared on Sally's desk. Lorne and Tony remained true to their word. They drank their coffee swiftly, shook hands with the team, wished them good luck, then headed back to London. Passing the beautiful flat, open countryside on the way had a calming effect over Lorne that she hadn't felt in years. She placed her hand on Tony's thigh while he drove. "Maybe we should consider retiring to this part of the world when we're old and grey, what do you think?"

"Why am I not surprised to hear you say that? Are you sure you wouldn't get bored?"

"Life is what you make it, Tony. You know that. We've both led pretty hectic lives to date. Perhaps going for a totally opposite lifestyle to what we have today would do us both the world of good. We could still renovate properties in our spare time."

"And that's what you call 'taking it easy'? You wouldn't be able to hand over the reins to a builder. You'd be knee-high in plaster and concrete within days of starting a new project. Don't you dare deny that, either."

Lorne looked out the passenger window and chortled. "You really do know me so well. Sometimes such bountiful knowledge is a huge disadvantage to me."

"That's true." He laughed.

Once they were back in London, Tony dropped Lorne off at the police station and continued home, promising to pick her up after work at around six.

Lorne appreciated her team's round of applause to welcome her back into the fold. Katy surprised her when she gave her a hug and a peck on the cheek. Lorne suspected her partner's hormones were to blame for her overly affectionate display. "I've missed you guys, too, but let's face it: it's only been a day."

"Do you want to grab a bite to eat first before we drive over to see Watts?" Katy asked, resting her backside on the nearest desk.

"Why not. Are you up to eating? You look a little pale."

"I'm fine. Nothing a Subway chicken tikka won't put right."

* * *

Replete, Lorne and Katy left the station around one thirty and arrived at Allan Watts's run-down flat approximately twenty minutes later. "Quite a contrast. Lucy's home in Norfolk is beautiful, a newly-renovated barn conversion on the river. It'll be interesting to see what he has to say and why he and the mysterious Claire Knight got divorced."

"You reckon he'll tell us?"

Lorne shrugged. "There's only one way to find out."

She rang the doorbell to the flat. A few minutes later, a grey-haired gentleman, who appeared to have just woken up, opened the door. His forehead creased as he peered at them. "Yes, can I help you?"

Lorne and Katy flashed their IDs under his nose. "DI Lorne Warner and DS Katy Foster. Do you mind if we come in for a chat, Mr. Watts?"

"About what?" he asked, rubbing at the stubble covering his chin as his frown deepened.

"Personal family business that I don't think your neighbours should hear about," Lorne replied, skirting the truth a little.

He sighed heavily. "I bet I can guess what 'family' you're referring to. You better come in."

Lorne and Katy followed him up the narrow passage, in need of repainting at the bottom, and through into the tiny open-plan living room cum kitchen, which was a total mess. There wasn't a clear surface in sight. Lorne gulped down the bile rising in her throat and regretted asking to speak to the man privately. Her heart went out to Katy, who looked as though she were about to regurgitate her lunch.

"Okay, hit me with it?" Watts prompted.

"We're dealing with a major crime and really only here to ask you about any background information you can give us regarding Claire Knight and her family," Lorne told him.

"In what respect? I'm not sure I'm the right person to be talking to if you want an unbiased opinion. You are aware that Claire and I got divorced earlier this year, right?"

"Yes, we're aware of that. Can you tell us why?"

"Why?"

"We're just trying to find out more about the family. While digging into Claire's background, some inaccuracies, shall we say, cropped up that we found rather puzzling, and we feel they need investigating further."

"Why come to me? To be honest with you, ladies, I can't stand the bloody woman, and to say I hope she rots in hell would be a gross understatement."

"Can you tell us why you hate her so much?" Lorne pressed.

"Look around you." His hand swept across the room. "This time last year, I was smugly tucked up in my mansion in Fulham. Can you imagine the humiliation I'm feeling at the moment?"

"It must be hard when your life is turned upside down like this. It would make us understand more if you could tell us why. Wasn't the house in your name?"

His chin sank to rest on his chest. "It was." He raised his head and shook it then raked a hand through his thinning hair. "Until she manipulated me into signing it over to her. She's an evil bitch. Mark my words when I tell you that. She'd sooner walk over you than around you to get what she wants in this life."

"If that's the case, why did you marry her? She must have had at least a few good qualities you admired before you proposed to her."

"Thinking back, I can't recall any. She employs tactics similar to what a conman would use to get money out of rich widows. Do you get where I'm coming from, Inspector?"

"I think I understand, yes. I'm sorry this has happened to you, Allan. Would you be prepared to help us more with our enquiries? It might go a long way to making up for the shame you've suffered at the hands of this woman." Lorne cringed at her words. However, by the way Allan was cringing himself, she knew she'd hit a nerve. Sometimes laying the facts out bare for folks spurred them to set off on their own journey of revenge. She'd used the ploy to great effect over the years.

"Nothing would give me greater satisfaction, Inspector. I'm just not sure my heart could stand the stress such activities would entail."

"Are you saying that you're in ill health, Allan?"

"I am. Which is why she pounced, I suspect. Unlike her other husbands, who are now both pushing up daisies, I had the courage to escape her treacherous clutches."

Lorne glanced at Katy and raised an eyebrow. "At a significant cost, it would seem," Lorne stated.

"Indeed. I have to ask what crime you're investigating, Inspector?"

"Murder," Lorne replied bluntly.

Allan's eyes widened. "Why am I not surprised to hear you say that? Would I know the person who has been murdered? Is that why you're here?" He gasped. "It's not *her*, is it?"

Lorne smiled. "No, it's not Claire Knight, although it is a member of her extended family. Ryan Timcott."

"Ryan! Jesus. How?"

"His boat exploded off the Kent coast on Sunday."

Allan shook his head in bemusement. "I wasn't aware he had a boat. What was he doing off the Kent coastline if he lives in Norfolk?"

"That's what we're trying to figure out. The boat was new. We have a few witnesses who have given us statements that Ryan left the marina with two women aboard his boat. However, only Ryan's body was found on the vessel."

"How strange. Forgive me if I'm missing something here, but how do you know it was murder and not just an unfortunate accident?"

"Because of the nature of Ryan's injuries—we can't go into details on that. Were you and Ryan close?"

"I've had business dealings with him in the past. Apart from meeting up at the odd family gathering, I wouldn't call us close."

"I see. Sorry, I should have asked what line of business you are in."

Seeming agitated, he began to pace the floor. "I was, before I met that confounded woman, in the banking business."

"And now?"

"How many bank managers do you know, Inspector, who live in squalor like this?"

"You've got me there. So what happened?"

"I got suspended, that's what. All because I fell in love with Claire Knight, or was it lust? I'm not sure. All I know is that she had some kind of spell over me."

"I'm sorry to hear that, Allan, but why the suspension?" Lorne hated urging the man to revisit his traumatic past, but she felt it was their best shot at delving into what made the woman tick.

He paused for a few seconds then responded with venom, "She wanted me to rob my own bank."

"What? And did you?"

"No. I would never do such an abysmal thing. I only had a few years to go before I received a substantial pension. It would have been foolish of me to jeopardise losing that after serving the bank for thirty years."

Lorne scratched the side of her face as she contemplated his answer. "So why did they suspend you? I'm confused."

"Because some kind soul, not mentioning any names, informed the bank of my intention. Only, nothing could be further from the truth."

"Claire? You think she dobbed you in?"

"Who else? She was livid when I refused to go along with her wishes. The bitch had it all meticulously planned out. If nothing else, she's an excellent planner."

"I don't suppose you can lay your hands on these plans? We could use it as evidence against her."

"No. I was that disgusted when she showed them to me, I threw them in the open fire. She was bloody furious. Came at me like a bloody madwoman. I'd never seen that side of her up until then."

"How long were you married, Allan?"

"Just over a year. The best and worst year of my life. We travelled to several exotic places I'd never dreamed of visiting before. I thought she truly loved me. Little did I know that she had ensnared me in her web and that her intentions would ultimately be of the unlawful variety. I'm a law-abiding citizen. I abhor any kind of deceit, Inspector. Now I've lost everything because I stupidly trusted and fell head over heels in love with a powerfully manipulative woman."

"I really am sorry that you got caught up with this woman. Wouldn't you feel better if you helped us bring her to justice?"

"Nothing would bring me greater pleasure, I assure you. But as I previously said, I doubt if my heart would take the stress. There's also the fact that she'll track me down somehow and finish me off. That was her parting words to me when she threw me out of my beautiful home. 'Divulge any of what this family gets up to, and your life won't be worth living.' I wouldn't put it past her to hire some kind of hitman to ensure that never happens."

"Really? She's that twisted?"

"Oh yes. Look, even if you offered me some kind of witness protection, I still wouldn't—and couldn't—help you. I couldn't stand the thought of having to look over my shoulder every second of the day, wondering what she would do if she ever tracked me down. I'd much rather live like this and stress-free. I realise the place is a shit-tip. One day, I'll get around to doing the right thing and clearing it up. I'm simply not in the right frame of mind at present. You understand that, don't you, ladies?"

Lorne rubbed his arm. "We understand. Sorry for the shit you've been caused by this woman. I can guarantee you one thing, Allan— we'll do our utmost to bring this woman to justice."

"Good luck with that, Inspector. I think you'll find it's not just Claire Knight you have to worry about. Her whole family are on the take in one way or another."

CHAPTER FOURTEEN

Olga Smitz snorted a line of coke and wiped away the excess powder from under her nose. She needed something to combat the fear and nerves churning up her insides like a washing machine on the full-spin cycle.

She was in position, sitting in the car outside the bank, following Teagan's instructions to the letter. All she could think about was what she would do with her 'payment.' She might have told her sisters a small fib about booking into rehab—she was still in two minds whether she wanted to go down that route or not. Her mind constantly swayed between wanting the euphoria of the drugs to continue and being fed up with snorting. She wanted a better life going forward.

A silver Merc entered the car park and pulled her out of her contemplative mood and sharply back to reality. She flashed her lights, and the driver of the Merc returned the gesture. The man, dressed in a steel grey suit and wearing a huge smile, walked towards her car. Actually, the car belonged to the family. Since the car was of little value it could be disposed of easily, which was likely after Olga had carried out Teagan's directives.

Olga forced herself to offer a welcoming smile as the man in his early thirties approached the car and snatched open the door. He fell into the passenger seat and nervously looked around him as his hand unfastened the zip on his trousers. Olga gulped. Teagan had prepared her that this man expected a blowjob as a form of introduction to working with someone new. The question was whether she had the stomach for obliging so early in the morning.

"Nice to meet you. Get on with it," he said, leaning back against the headrest after exposing his mediocre-sized manhood.

Thankfully, the effects of the coke hit her just as she lowered her head to his lap. Every time a groan of satisfaction left his mouth, she had to resist the temptation to bite down hard on his dick. With the task completed, and feeling sick to the stomach, she sat up and wiped her mouth on the sleeve of her jumper.

"You're good," he stated, his eyes focused on the stray drip she'd unfortunately missed at the side of her mouth.

Another swipe across her lips dealt with the offending liquid. "Well, do you have it?"

The man laughed and zipped up his trousers. "No chance of doing that again, I suppose?"

"You're right—there's no chance of that. Teagan said she thought you'd try it on, so she gave me your wife's number." Olga picked up her mobile. Her thumb hovered mischievously over the dial button. "It's programmed in. All I need to do is hit the button. Cut the crap and give me what you're supposed to deliver, and be quick about it. Do you want your staff showing up and seeing what you get up to when you're not treating them like shit at work?"

"That's where you're wrong. I treat my staff very well indeed," he countered, obviously offended.

"Especially the female ones, eh? You probably hold frequent meetings in your office and receive regular favours. Don't bother denying it, either. The world is crammed-full of guys like you." Olga eyed him with contempt, regretting her actions immediately. It was the drugs talking. If Teagan found out, her life wouldn't be worth living, not that it was up to much anyway.

He placed his hand on the door handle and glared at her. "That's easily corrected. I don't have to take this kind of bullshit from you or any other member of your family. You can go whistle for your money now." If he thought his words would scare her, he was gravely mistaken. Olga hit the dial key and put her phone on speaker. A scuffle broke out as he tried to snatch the phone from her hand before his wife answered the call. "You crazy fucking bitch, give me the damn phone."

The car fell silent when his wife's frustrated tone filled the car. "Hello? Hello? Who is this? Go play your stupid pranks on someone else, you cocksucker!" The line went dead.

Olga sniggered. "She must have a crystal ball." Her smile quickly turned into a sneer. "Next time, I'll talk and tell her how accurate her name-calling was. Now, do I have your full attention?"

"You're bloody sick. You wait, your sister will be hearing about your fucking stunt."

"Yeah, yeah. Just bloody hand over the money and papers, and I'll get out of your hair."

He shook his head. "It's not going to happen. I draw the line at working with psychos."

Olga hit the send button again on the phone. "Your choice, buster. Wanna make a bet on how little wifey is going to react when she hears what a naughty boy you've been?"

"All right, you've made your bloody point. Hang up, and I'll go and get what you need from the car."

"I knew a little coercion would make you see sense. Hop to it, before your staff turn up."

He exited the car and raced back to his own. Shiftily scanning the area around him, he ran back to the car and threw a carrier bag at her. Olga needed to think quickly to prevent him from leaving the car. A huge smile pulled her lips apart to show her beautifully white teeth, then she seductively ran her tongue across her lips. "There's a good boy. That's deserving of an encore, don't you think?"

He didn't hesitate. He stumbled into the passenger seat again and unzipped his trousers. Olga gulped down the bile rising in her throat, and while one hand reached for his limp cock, her other hand felt under her seat for the weapon. She had no intention of letting him near her mouth again, but she did have other plans for his now-erect penis.

CHAPTER FIFTEEN

Lorne and Katy arrived at the station in a thoughtful mood that soon dispersed once AJ filled them in on a new case. The body of a man had been found in a bank's car park.

"What? Out in the open? In the daylight? Not disguised at all?" Lorne asked incredulously, thinking AJ was talking about a murder victim, judging by the injuries he'd relayed to them.

"Nope. Just ditched near his car."

"I take it the pathologist is at the scene, AJ?"

"Yes, boss."

"Right, do you want to come with me, Katy, or would you rather stay here?"

"Maybe I'll pass the baton to AJ on this one. Would you mind?" Katy asked, looking from Lorne to her fiancé.

AJ shrugged. "Fine by me."

"That's settled, then. Grab your coat."

AJ raced down the stairs behind Lorne and out of the station. The bank was situated in Fulham, at least a forty-minute drive away. Weariness seeped through her veins after the long drive she'd experienced with Tony that morning, but her determination to get to the scene ASAP spurred her on.

Patti was at her car, searching for something in the boot when they drew up at the zoned-off crime scene. "Everything all right, Patti? This is AJ, Katy's fiancé. Not sure if you've ever had the pleasure of meeting him before."

Patti looked AJ up and down and whistled. "Katy is a *very* lucky girl, and I predict that baby she's carrying is going to break hearts with a handsome couple like you being its parents."

Lorne thumbed in Patti's direction. "As you can see, Patti has never been the type of person to hold back." Lorne laughed when she saw the colour rise in AJ's cheeks. "Aww… look what you've done, Patti."

Patti dug around in her car and mumbled, "I know what I'd like to do to him."

Lorne placed her hand over her eyes and chuckled. Pulling a straight face, she asked, "Do we have a clue who the victim is yet?"

After retrieving a few evidence bags from the boot, Patti turned and led the way back to the body covered by a sheet close to his car.

"Yep, he was identified earlier as Daniel Grade, the bank manager of this branch."

"What? Did a member of his staff find him?" Lorne glanced up at the building to see if she could locate any CCTV cameras.

"Yes, a few of them turned up for work in a car-share and discovered the gruesome find." Patti crouched and pulled back the sheet to reveal the victim's upper torso.

"Ouch!" Lorne said as AJ gasped. "Let's hope he was dead before it was cut off."

Patti glanced up at Lorne and shook her head slowly. "Nope. This man suffered a significant amount of pain and blood loss before his death. He has a nick to his femoral artery. The combined injuries would have been enough to kill him fairly quickly. Someone had a personal score to settle, don't you think?"

"Agreed. The intent was pretty vicious, then."

"Maybe he was cheating on his wife," AJ offered, wincing.

Lorne tilted her head from side to side, observing the man's penis emerging from his own mouth. "You're probably right with that conjecture, AJ. The first thing we need to accomplish is seeing if the CCTV system was functioning last night. I'll leave you to deal with that, AJ, as it seems to be your forte."

AJ left them and walked into the bank.

"Any form of evidence found yet, Patti?" Lorne asked.

"Not that I can tell, except..."

"Go on? Stop your bloody teasing."

"Well, I took an initial sample from the man's penis, and my preliminary assessment would be that he's recently had sex, maybe not vaginal sex. I think we're more than likely talking about oral sex."

"So, he had oral sex with someone in a car park, and then that person chopped his dick off and shoved it in his mouth! An unsatisfied lover? A prostitute perhaps? Is his wallet still on him?"

"Yes, his wallet is here. As to your other theories, I wouldn't like to say. My opinion is you're dealing with someone not quite right in the head."

"Der... obviously! What about a staff member? Maybe he was having an affair with a colleague and he tried to call it off."

"That's your department, Lorne. I'm only here to gather the evidence to put before you."

"And a mighty fine job you do of that, too."

Patti re-covered the corpse and stood up. "I'm actually surprised to see you here. What about your other case? The boat explosion? How's that progressing?"

"It's turning out to be far more complicated than we ever expected. Tony and I have just returned from Norfolk this morning."

"Really? Why is Tony involved?"

"He's not. I wanted moral support. Truth be told, I didn't want to make the long trip by myself. The good news is that one of my dear friends, DI Sally Parker of the Norfolk Constabulary, is working the case at that end."

Patti frowned. "A joint investigation? How come?"

"Because of where the victim, Ryan Timcott, was based. It's still puzzling us why he travelled down here with his boat. According to his wife, he was out showing off his new acquisition to his mates, who are all based in the Norfolk area. Sally intends to question Ryan's friends over the next few days. In the meantime, my suspicions lie at the mother-in-law's door. She seems an evil cow, grossly lacking in compassion for her daughter's grief, from what I could tell."

"How strange. Are you saying that you think the mother was one of the women aboard the boat?"

"At this point, I really couldn't say. However, we're coming up with some very interesting information that we found lingering in her dark past."

"Interesting information? Anything I can help you with?" Patti offered.

"Possibly. I want to discover all the facts I can about her previous marriages first, and then I might take you up on your offer. Two of her husbands died in suspicious circumstances, and the recent one is living in squalor while she lives it up in a mansion which belonged to him long before she came on the scene. He didn't have a good thing to say about Claire Knight, if I'm honest. I'm sure it wasn't a case of sour grapes, either."

Patti nodded at the corpse. "Looks like you and your team are going to have your hands full over the coming few weeks."

"It does indeed. You could help us out by rushing the PM and path tests through on matey here, if you'd be so kind?" Lorne winked at her friend.

"Ever the one to pour pressure on me, aren't you? I'll do my best."

"Have you done anything about obtaining DNA from the staff?"

"Do you want me to? What about a warrant?"

"Bear with me two minutes. If the staff members have nothing to hide, then in my opinion, they'll be willing to offer us a sample of their DNA."

"You're a crafty mare at times, Lorne Warner."

"Just doing my job, Patti." Lorne marched into the bank, which was temporarily closed to the public, to find three women and a young man talking to AJ. Lorne introduced herself and said, "I'm truly sorry for your loss. Who found the victim?"

The young man raised his hand. "Tanya and me. He was just lying there, covered in blood. I rang 999 immediately and ushered Tanya inside."

"Are you up to answering some questions?" Lorne's heart felt heavy as she observed the tortured expressions of the staff.

"Of course, we want the person who did this caught as soon as possible," the young man said.

"That's our aim too. Sorry, I didn't catch your name?"

"It's Nigel Manning. I'm the assistant bank manager."

"I take it that you've informed head office of the incident?"

"Yes, directly after I rang 999, I called my area manager."

"I wonder if any of you would object to giving us a DNA sample? It's more to eliminate people from our enquiries early on than anything." Lorne clarified when Nigel looked shocked by her request.

"I have no objection to that, Inspector. Does anyone else?" he asked the three stunned women, who all responded by shaking their heads.

"Wonderful. Maybe there's an office we can use for privacy? It'll only be a buccal swab."

"Yes, my office," he replied without hesitation.

Over the next half an hour, Lorne and AJ jotted down each of the staff's statements and took the DNA samples. Before leaving the bank, they also obtained a copy of the CCTV disc, though Lorne was dubious whether it would offer much in the way of clues because of its positioning in the car park. She was more hopeful that one of the cameras on the side or front of the building might highlight a strange vehicle in the vicinity that morning. That was their first priority once they returned to the station. But in the meantime, Lorne had the daunting task of visiting the victim's wife and sharing the sad news of her husband's untimely demise.

Lorne parked outside the large home on a main thoroughfare into the heart of Fulham. She admired the Georgian façade of the imposing two-storey terraced house, aware of the high costs involved in purchasing and running a house in such an affluent area. "Are you ready for this?" she asked AJ.

"The least pleasant part of the job, eh?"

"Just leave the talking to me, and you'll be fine."

AJ did the honours of ringing the doorbell. A woman in her early thirties opened the door. In her arms was a small child of around eighteen months.

Lorne gulped and flashed her ID at the woman. "Mrs. Sonia Grade? I'm DI Lorne Warner, and this is my partner, DS Alan Jackson from the Met Police. Is it possible to come in for a moment to speak to you?"

Mrs. Grade seemed puzzled. "I'm sorry, what is this about? I have a clinic to attend with the little one shortly. I don't wish to be rude, but I don't want to be late for the appointment, either. They're like gold dust."

"It is important. Please, it would be better inside." Lorne smiled, and the woman reluctantly stepped aside to allow them to enter her beautiful home.

After closing the front door, she swept past them and into the large lounge. She placed the child into a playpen in the corner of the room and sat down in the easy chair next to it.

Lorne inhaled a deep breath before she began talking.

The woman raised a questioning eyebrow at Lorne's delay.

"I'm sorry. There's no easy way of telling you this, Mrs. Grade. I regret to inform you that your husband died this morning." Lorne lowered her voice when she mentioned the husband's death in case the child understood what was being said.

The woman's hand covered her mouth, and a sob escaped her throat. "What?" she whispered after a few seconds.

"Maybe it would be better if we called a member of your family to be with you, to look after the child while we speak?"

"Yes." She extracted her mobile phone from her handbag next to the sofa and rang someone. "Mum, can you come over? Please… don't ask me to tell you over the phone. Just get here, quickly." She hung up. "Mum lives around the corner. She'll be with us in a few minutes. Is that okay?"

"Of course."

A strained silence filled the room; only the child's happy chortles could be heard.

Moments later, the front door opened and slammed shut, then a slim lady dressed in an olive-green trouser suit entered the room. "Hello. Who's this, sweetheart?"

Lorne flashed her ID again and introduced herself.

"Police? What's this in connection with? Should my grandchild be in the room to hear this?"

"It's Daniel, Mum. They say he was found dead this morning."

Lorne saw the colour drain from the mother's face and then asked her to take a seat. "I'm sorry. I didn't catch your name?"

Looking stunned, she replied, "Janet Falk. Oh my goodness, how?"

"I was just about to explain the circumstances to your daughter but was conscious about your grandchild overhearing the facts."

"But I should be here when you tell her, for support. Can't he look after Amelia for a few minutes?" Mrs. Falk asked, pointing at AJ.

Lorne looked at her partner. "Would that be okay with you, AJ?"

"Sure, it'll be good practice." He approached the playpen as Sonia stood and picked up the child again.

"I'll settle her into the highchair; you can watch over her there, if that's okay?"

AJ left the room with Sonia and Amelia. Mrs. Falk's gaze landed on Lorne through narrowed eyes as she asked, "Was he held up at the bank?"

"No, it was nothing like that. The incident happened outside his workplace."

The lounge door opened, and Sonia walked back into the room and sat down. "How did it happen?"

"As I've just explained to your mother, Daniel's body was found outside the bank. He never made it into work this morning."

"What? Did someone hijack him to gain access to the bank?"

Lorne shook her head. "We don't think so, although we could be wrong. A Forensics team are at the scene investigating all the possibilities." She cleared her throat and continued. "I have to ask if anything suspicious has occurred in your husband's life lately? By that I mean, has anyone contacted him? Threatened him? Tried to coerce him into doing something detrimental to his reputation?"

Sonia frowned and glanced at her mother. "Is she asking if Daniel was possibly on the take, Mum?"

"I don't know, dear," Janet replied. She turned to face Lorne. "Are you? Is that what you think this is about? I know how risky it is being a bank manager these days. They're perceived as being a soft touch to gain easy money."

Lorne swallowed hard. She didn't really want to deceive the women any longer than necessary. "You're not going to like what I have to tell you. However, I think you should know the full facts concerning your husband's death, Sonia."

"You're worrying me, Inspector. Please, come right out with it. I'd rather know from the outset what the facts are."

A quick assessment told Lorne that she felt the woman could handle the horrific truth. "Very well. Your husband was found murdered, lying in a pool of blood in the rear car park at the bank. Unfortunately, his attacker cut off part of his anatomy. To date, we can't tell you the significance behind such actions. Usually an injury of this kind implies that the assailant has been intimate with the victim in some way. In this instance, the nature of that intimacy is yet to be ascertained."

"I don't understand. What are you telling me? What part of him has been removed?"

Lorne sighed heavily and held the woman's gaze with her own. "His penis."

Sonia broke down, and her mother rushed to be by her side.

"What kind of perverse world are we living in, Inspector? Why would anyone do that to another human being? Why?" Janet whispered as if voicing the words too loudly would double her daughter's pain.

"I don't know, but I'm certainly going to do my utmost to find out. Has your husband mentioned anything out of the ordinary happening at work, Sonia?"

"No, nothing that I can recall. My head is all over the place right now." She stared at her daughter's playpen, her eyes narrowing as she thought.

"Have you thought of something, Sonia? It doesn't matter if you think it's insignificant. At this moment, we have very little to go on, so any clues you might give us could help us to solve the case quicker."

"Something jumped into my mind. I was getting Amelia's breakfast ready this morning when the phone rang. I thought it was a prank call. The caller listened but refused to say anything."

"About what time?" Lorne withdrew her notebook from her pocket.

Sonia's hand touched her temple. "I don't know. I suppose around eight fifteen to eight thirty. I got annoyed with the caller. They caught me at the wrong time because Amelia had just spilt her cereal over the floor. I shouted down the line and called them an unsavoury name."

Lorne smiled. "You're entitled to if it was indeed a nuisance call. And they said nothing at all?"

"No. Do you think there's a connection? Did my outburst cause my husband's death?" Sonia broke down again.

"Please, you mustn't think that, Sonia. We're unsure how or what took place at present. It might have been a hostage situation gone wrong for all we know. The speculation could be endless until we get the clarification we need from the pathologist. Her report should be back within the next few days."

"Can I see him?" Sonia asked, apparently willing to accept Lorne's statement.

"Of course, but that won't be allowed to take place before the postmortem has been performed. The pathology department will contact you directly, to give you the option and times when visits are permitted."

"Thank you. Will I recognise him? Was he badly beaten also?"

"No, there was barely a scratch on him, except for the injuries we've already discussed. Would you mind if I took a look at your phone? Is the number still registered, or did you delete it?"

Sonia picked up her mobile and handed it to Lorne. "I didn't have time to delete the number. It should still be registered as the last call received."

Lorne jotted down the digits. She was tempted to redial the number but thought better of it. If the call had come from the murderer, the last thing she wanted to do was tip the person off. "Hopefully, this will lead us to the guilty party. It's a start anyway."

"So you think you'll be able to trace the person using the number?" Janet asked hopefully.

"Providing they haven't dumped the phone by now. That's a distinct possibility, especially if they've realised how foolish it was to ring Sonia. If indeed it was the murderer who called. There are always a lot of what-if scenarios we have to chase during an investigation, but they all tend to come together and point us in the right direction, in the end."

"Do you need anything else, Inspector? I'd like to take care of my daughter now," Janet said, patting Sonia's hand.

"I think that's it, except to express my sincere condolences and to assure you that I will do everything in my power to bring this person to justice."

"I hope so. How will I cope without Daniel?" Sonia cried and buried her head in her hands.

"I know it's a bit of a cliché, Sonia, but time is a great healer. Obtaining justice can also ensure that healing is achieved more quickly. Did your husband have life insurance? Is the house on a mortgage?"

"Yes, he had insurance, and yes, we have a *huge* mortgage."

"I'm sure the insurance will cover it. I know it's not nice discussing such matters, but there is still a need for practicality going forward, if only to give you peace of mind. Perhaps leave it a few days for things to sink in." Lorne rose from her seat and walked towards the lounge door. "I'll collect my partner and shoot off, if that's all right?"

Both women followed her into the hallway. Sonia went ahead to rescue AJ from Amelia's playful antics.

As soon as AJ re-joined Lorne, they left the grieving women and returned to the station.

CHAPTER SIXTEEN

Claire left Lucy's house in Norfolk around mid-morning. Grinning, she drove back down to London, happy to be away from the drab existence of country life and looking forward to going out that evening on the social scene at a plush restaurant, not that she could afford it. She would need to do what she always did: entice a member of the opposite sex to pay for her meal. The ploy had worked thousands of times over the years. She had no reason to believe that night would be any different. In her experience, men often went to restaurants and sat at the bar, waiting to pounce on what they thought was easy prey. She had tempted many a desperate man with her beauty and her flirtatious nature, leading them to think that dessert would be on offer at a nearby hotel, only to do a runner at the restaurant once the bill appeared. She had a gift that would stand her in good stead for years, providing she kept her looks and her slim figure intact.

Claire pulled into her drive and was surprised to see Olga sitting on the granite steps of her home, looking like some kind of vagrant. The only thing missing from the scene was a begging bowl. "Olga? What are you doing here?"

"Can't a daughter visit her mother now and again without getting the third degree?"

Claire eyed her with contempt. She hated it when her children disrespected her, even more so when that daughter was her youngest, and a shameful drug addict to boot. "You look like shit. If I get my hands on your bloody dealer, I'm going to shove him in a wood chipper. You're a disgrace to this family."

"Thanks, Ma. I had a feeling I wouldn't get the support I needed here. I never have in the past; why should today be any different? I'll leave you to your world of grandeur and snobbiness and take my drug-filled sorry arse out of here."

"Stop your whining, child, and get indoors before the sodding neighbours lay eyes on you." Claire hauled her daughter to her feet and looked down at her bloody hand in horror. "What the?"

"I didn't intend to do it, I swear. Everything just snowballed, and before I knew what was happening, it was too late to back out."

"Inside. Don't say anything else until we're on the other side of the door." She shoved her daughter in the back and wiped her blood-soaked hand down Olga's sweatshirt.

Once the door was closed, Claire folded her arms and cocked her head to the side. "Well?"

Olga's foot circled the marble hall floor a few times as if she were searching for the courage to speak.

Claire growled and stomped off into the living room, where she felt most at home, surrounded by the luxurious swag-and-tail brocade curtains, plus all the antiques her former husband had lovingly collected over the years and left behind after the divorce. Claire sat down in the high-backed Queen Anne chair and crossed her arms. "I'm waiting. You have precisely five minutes to tell me what has gone on, or…" She deliberately left the sentence unfinished. She'd learnt over the years that those kinds of threats had far more success. Olga went to sit down on the fabric sofa, but Claire shouted, "Don't you dare."

Olga glared. "That phrase has been directed at me more often than anyone else in this family. Maybe if you'd treated me with more compassion, I wouldn't be in this mess now."

"What are you referring to with that sweeping statement? Your drug addict status? Or the fact that it looks like you've just ended someone's life? You make me sick. Yes, I'm guilty of saying 'don't you dare' more to you than any of my other children, but I'm also guilty of spoiling you more than the others. I blame myself for giving you far too much money over the years, money that you've seen fit to waste on filthy drugs. Why? Why have you turned to that disgusting habit? None of the others have. Why you?"

"The need to suppress the feelings of hate towards you and the rest of the family is a considerable factor, Mother."

Claire's temper rose. "And you think telling me that is going to transfer the guilt you're feeling onto me? Is that it? I'm assuring you, Olga, it isn't. You're despicable. Tell me what you've done. Now!"

Olga started to walk back and forth in front of her. "Teagan asked me to carry out a job for her."

"Let me stop you right there. Since when does Teagan give the orders around here?"

Olga shrugged. "I don't know."

"Was there money involved?"

Olga's hand covered her eyes before her bitten fingernails tried to scratch her face. "Yes, fifty thousand."

Claire shot out of her chair, grabbed her daughter's shoulders, and shook them violently. "What? Where the hell did she get that kind of money?" Claire was furious. She'd been rubbing pennies together for the past few months, trying to think of numerous ways to supplement her income, only to hear that her eldest child is bandying around tens of thousands of pounds.

Olga tensed up and tried to struggle out of her mother's grip. "I don't know, Ma. Don't frigging have a go at me. I did what I was asked to do."

Claire pushed her daughter away, furious about her family's deceit. "I'm the one who gives the orders, and do you know why that is? No? Then I'll tell you—because I'm the one with the brains. This week alone, Teagan has messed up more times than I have in all the decades I've been doing this. What bothers me the most is the rest of you are so willing to go along with her plans—plans that are doomed to failure because of her lack of insight. Out with it, who have you killed and why?"

"I don't want this shit. All I wanted was to make some easy money. There's no way I'm going to get caught up in the middle of this."

Laughing, Claire pointed in her daughter's face. "I think you'll find it's too late to start saying things like that, my girl. Tell me!"

Olga took a few steps back and began pacing once more, tugging at the roots of her hair.

Claire walked towards the phone and picked it up. "Do I have to ring Teagan myself?"

"No! Don't do that. I should have reported back to her once I'd completed the task, but I came straight here instead."

"Why? Because you thought I would dig you out of a hole? You expect me to make things right when you're prepared to go behind my back like this? You're crazier than I thought. Either tell me or get the fuck out of this house now. My patience for your drug-related behaviour ran out years ago."

Olga sighed heavily. "Teagan is going to kill me when she finds out."

"It's *me* you should be worried about, not *Teagan*. I'll bloody kill you if you don't reveal what you've done, Olga. And believe me, that's not an idle threat."

"Jesus, Mother!"

Claire placed the phone back in its docking station and crossed her arms. Her foot tapped impatiently as she waited for her daughter to come to her senses and tell her what bizarre plan the two sisters had concocted.

"I want to sit down. My legs are going to give way any minute."

"I've heard some pretty lame excuses come out of your mouth, but that tops the lot. *Get on with it!*"

Olga began to cry.

Claire's heart had been hardened to her daughter's ability to break down into tears when she craved sympathy. She remained quiet and continued tapping her foot.

"You're a hard bitch! A mother is supposed to be kind and gentle to her offspring, not like you. Sometimes I think all maternal instincts were stripped from you once all of our umbilical cords were cut. I hate you!"

"The feeling's mutual at times, I can bloody assure you. Now, get out of my house and don't ever darken my doorstep again!"

Olga's eyes widened, and her jaw slackened to reveal her teeth. "What? But where will I go? Who will get me out of this mess?"

"You should have thought about that before you started slinging shit at me. Go back to your sister with these words: 'Two fuck-ups in a week will land you all in deep trouble. Don't bother coming to me for any advice or help.' You two are on your own from now on. I'm publicly washing my hands of you. Now, let's see how long it takes for one of you to end up in prison."

"But Mum…"

Claire shook her head and pointed at the front door. "Out!"

"What about the funeral? We can't fall out before Ryan's funeral. Lucy needs our support."

"Lucy will have my support. It's the rest of you who need to realise what I do for this family. Between you, you've darkened my name once too often, and I'm sure you'll be guilty of leading the police to my door. I don't take stupidity like that lightly. Keep your secrets between you—that's your prerogative. Just don't turn up on my doorstep expecting me to get you out of the shit. Pass the message on."

Claire walked out of the room and made her way upstairs. She stood at the top and strained her ear, waiting to hear the front door close behind her daughter. Once she heard the slam of the door, she continued along the landing and into her bedroom, where she proceeded to fill the bath. In times of stress, only a deep bubble bath would suffice. It also helped her to think. She had a feeling her bath would be refilled with hot water numerous times as she hatched plans to get herself out of her dire financial straits. The mess that Olga had brought to her door didn't even enter her mind. The rest of her family could go to hell. She would have no hesitation in sticking by Lucy, however. She was the only one who had ever shown Claire any form of loyalty in recent years.

CHAPTER SEVENTEEN

Lorne travelled back to Norfolk alone to attend the funeral of Ryan Timcott with Sally. She pulled into the police station car park and announced herself at the front desk. A few moments later, Sally came to collect her and took her to the incident room.

Sally ran through the information she and her team had gathered about Lucy and her family since Lorne's departure. "That's it really at this end," Sally said, standing next to the incident board. "Nothing that exciting to go on. None of Ryan's friends knew he even had a boat, let alone went aboard to take a gander. I did, however, find out one thing that could prove to be interesting."

"What's that?" Lorne asked, intrigued.

"Ryan took out a secured loan for the boat against the property."

"Hmm... you're thinking that Lucy doesn't know about this?"

"Exactly. I think she would've mentioned it."

"Maybe. Let's give her the benefit of the doubt. She appeared to be riddled with grief. What about his background check into his finances? Any other surprises there?"

"We're still looking. A few insignificant oddities, but nothing major from what we can gather. Any joy at your end?"

"It's tricky, and as far as Claire Knight is concerned, *she's* tricky. I managed to visit her latest ex last week. He's an extremely bitter man and rightly so. My take is that she's blackmailing him in some way, although he wouldn't come out and say it."

"Blackmail? That points at him having something to hide."

Lorne nodded thoughtfully. "That's my assumption. He lost his job because of an anonymous phone call to the head office of the bank where he worked. Do you think both Ryan Timcott and Allan Watts being involved in the finance industry has anything to do with this case? Should Allan feel relieved that he's escaped with his life intact, or is that me blowing things out of perspective?"

"We'll need to keep digging into that side of things. Let's see what the funeral throws up today and go from there."

Lorne agreed, and they drove to the little church in Horning, where the service was being held.

"Well, there's Claire. Am I imagining things, or does she appear to be glaring at some of the other family members?" Lorne asked as Sally brought the car to a halt and switched off the engine.

"Looks that way to me. The other girls are all together, and the mother seems keen on keeping her distance from them. Do you think they've fallen out? It's not unheard of at funerals."

"Possibly. I'm dying to find out." Lorne got out of the car and stopped before she closed the passenger door. She spotted a man in in his mid-thirties, wearing a black coat, standing close to Claire. "Interesting... I wonder who he is?"

Sally followed Lorne's gaze. "Her next conquest perhaps."

They both chuckled. "Quaking at the thought of that, given the difference in their ages. Not that it matters with today's cougar generation."

Lorne and Sally approached Claire, hoping to get an introduction, but as soon as she realised they were heading her way, she linked arms with the man and steered him in the opposite direction, away from the gathering crowd. "Interesting. Little does she realise what she's done by doing that. Let's play it cool for now, give her the space she needs. We'll pounce on them when she's least expecting it."

"I agree. Not the wisest move she's ever made."

Lucy smiled when she saw Lorne and Sally walking towards her. She held out her hand for them to shake. "I'm so pleased you could make it. I was hoping you might have some good news regarding my husband's case."

"Sadly not, Lucy. We'll have a private chat afterwards. We just wanted to offer our condolences to you all." Lorne turned to the other members of the group and smiled. She was hoping that Lucy or one of the others would introduce everyone who was present—they didn't. "I'm sorry. You are?"

Lucy bashed the side of her head with the palm of her hand. "Where are my manners? These are my three sisters, Teagan, Helen, and Olga."

Lorne smiled briefly at the sisters. "Pleased to meet you. Sorry for your loss." She looked behind her and asked Lucy, "I have to ask, is your mother okay?"

Lucy glanced through the crowd at her mother. "Yes, she's just catching up with Joe. He's our brother. He lives up in Manchester, so we don't see him much."

"Yeah and Mother seems intent on keeping him all to herself," Olga complained, glaring in her mother's direction.

"Am I sensing some animosity between you all?" Lorne asked.

"No! Nothing of the sort," Teagan replied before adding sharply, "If you'll excuse us, we're needed in the church now."

With that, the group disappeared inside the church. Lorne looked over her shoulder at Claire. "Well, she doesn't seem to be in any rush to get inside. I can't say she looks happy to be chatting to her son, either."

"Are you surprised? This family's antics get weirder by the day. Shall we go in or wait outside until everyone is seated?"

"I'd rather observe things from inside. Anyway, it'll be warmer in there than out here."

They entered the church and sat in the last pew on the right. Lorne's gaze remained glued to the group of sisters. She was aware her presence could possibly trigger someone into making a foolish mistake, if they were guilty of anything.

Over the next five minutes, the crowd filtered into the church and found seats. Lorne was surprised to see Claire and her son enter the church at the rear of all the other mourners. Claire pulled on her son's arm when he attempted to sit next to his siblings. His mother led him to a pew at the front, on the opposite side to the rest of the family. Sally nudged Lorne and pointed at Claire's daughter Teagan, whose annoyance oozed from every pore. "Looks like that particular move hasn't gone down well."

Lorne placed her hand up to her face and whispered behind it, "There's an obvious rift. What we need to find out is what has caused such a split in the family. Maybe after the service, you can think of a way to distract the mother long enough for me to grab a quick word with her son."

"Sure, if I can. She strikes me as being super cute. There's every possibility I might fail in that task."

"Do your best. I'm going to try and organise a meeting with him later."

After the lengthy service had concluded, the crowd followed the family out of the church and milled around outside in the car park, apparently at a loss for what to do next. Lorne seized her opportunity to talk to Joe Knight when a couple in their sixties started speaking to Claire. Swooping like a bird of prey, she tapped Joe on the shoulder and extended her hand.

"Hi, Joe, please forgive the intrusion. I'm DI Lorne Warner from the Met in London. I'm the investigating officer in your brother-in-law's murder."

His eyes darted in his mother's direction, then he surprised Lorne by grabbing her by the elbow and leading her a few feet away, out of his mother's earshot. "I can't talk here."

"Why? Because of your mother?"

"Yes. I'm staying at the Innkeeper's Lodge in Horning. Can you drop by this evening to see me? I'd do it sooner, as I'm keen to speak with you, but I'll have to show my face at the wake this afternoon. Shall we say at seven this evening? I have to go. Mother is watching us." Apparently for his mother's benefit, he raised his voice and said, "I'm sorry I can't help you. I'm not from around here. Goodbye."

Lorne resisted the urge to shudder under Claire Knight's vicious gaze, which ended only once her son was safely standing alongside her.

Sally turned her back and chuckled. "That's a pretty nasty stare she's intent on aiming at us. Anyone would think we're the enemy instead of trying to do our best to help her. I'd love to know what her problem is."

"Let's hope Joe can shed some light on that later. Will you be able to accompany me to the hotel this evening?"

"Of course. You better stay overnight with me again."

"I don't want to put you and your parents out, Sally."

"You won't be."

That evening, Lorne and Sally remained at the station until six thirty then drove to the hotel where Joe was staying.

He was waiting for them in the reception area. "Thank you for coming. Shall we go through to the bar?"

Lorne and Sally shook his hand then followed him into the hotel's bar. It was empty except for a giggling man and woman sitting at the bar. They calmed down the instant Lorne and Sally entered.

"What would you like to drink, ladies?" the barman enquired.

"Orange juice will be fine for me," Lorne replied with a smile.

"Sounds good to me, and another drink for our friend." Sally pointed at Joe.

The barman prepared the drinks and placed them on the polished wooden bar before pouring a pint of lager for Joe.

Once they were settled at a table by the window, avoiding any unnecessary small talk, Lorne asked, "What can you tell us, Joe?" Lorne noticed the redness surrounding his eyes. *Has he been crying before we got here?*

He picked up his drink, and his hand shook uncontrollably, causing him to spill some of it on the table. "Damn! What do you want to know, Inspector?"

Lorne smiled, trying to reassure him that he'd done the right thing calling a meeting with them. "Anything and everything. How's that? You live in Manchester, is that right?"

Replacing his glass on the table, he reclined in his chair. "Yes. I left the London area years ago."

"Any particular reason?" Sally withdrew her notebook from her handbag and opened it to a clean page.

"Let's just say that I was eager to leave my mother's clutches as soon as I could."

"Well, that statement has certainly sparked our interest, Joe. Care to share why?" Lorne took a sip of her orange juice as the inside of her mouth dried up with the anticipation.

Joe inhaled and exhaled a few deep breaths, and his gaze drifted out the window. Lorne winked at Sally. A final sigh left his body before he continued, "His screams still haunt me. They fill my dreams and turn them into nightmares." He fell silent again.

Lorne placed a hand over his. "Take your time, Joe. There's no rush."

"I've lived with this torment for years. He didn't deserve to die, not like that. *She* did it."

Her hand squeezed his. "We'll do all we can to ease your pain if you'll confide in us, Joe. Who died? Who is she? Your mother?"

His gaze met Lorne's, and he nodded as his eyes moistened with tears. "There's only one word to describe my mother, ladies: Evil."

"We haven't discovered much about your mother's past yet, but from what we can gather, that word pretty much sums her up accurately. My partner and I visited your ex-stepfather in London last week. He was far from complimentary about your mother, understandably so, in the circumstances. Did you get on well with him?"

"To be honest, I didn't really know him. Over the years, I've had less and less to do with my family."

"Sorry to hear that, Joe. If that's the case, can I ask why you turned up for the funeral today?" Lorne asked.

"I see weddings and funerals as a duty, nothing more."

"Did you go to your mother's last wedding? I'm only asking because you just said that you barely knew Allan."

"Yes, I attended the wedding, but I kept my distance. That has always been expected of me."

Lorne frowned. "What? To keep your distance?"

He took another sip of his drink. "My mother has always preferred the girls to surround her, which suits me, Inspector, especially after I witnessed that tragic event."

"Are you referring to the person who died? Who was that, Joe?"

His hands covered his eyes, and a sob escaped his mouth. Then he whispered, "My father."

Lorne's eyes widened. When she looked in Sally's direction, her eyes were as round as plates, too. Recovering quickly from the revelation, Lorne asked, "I know how hard this must be for you, but we'd really appreciate it if you would share with us what happened."

Joe remained quiet for the next few moments.

"Joe, we've delved into your mother's background and are aware that two of her husbands have died in suspicious circumstances. Did she kill them? Is that how your father died?"

His breathing came in short bursts.

Lorne covered his hand with hers again. "Please, Joe, tell us. Help us to right a very bad wrong."

"He came towards me. I was five at the time. My mother hated me. Nowadays, she tolerates me, and that's all I can say about our relationship. My sisters are the same. I'm treated as an outcast only because I had the guts to leave the family home as soon as I was old enough."

"You said he came towards you; in what respect?" Sally asked quietly.

"Mum and dad were arguing, as usual. I heard them going at it downstairs, but somehow, this sounded different to the others they'd had, more intense, I suppose. I crept downstairs and watched the proceedings through the spindles midway on the stairs. She started throwing things at him, aiming at his head. One particular pot shattered on his forehead; I remember that so clearly. My father dropped to the ground, blood seeping from the wound to his head. Did she care? No! She continued to throw all she could find at him. He tried several attempts to get to his feet, but it was hopeless. I saw her pick up the lamp and knew then that her intention was to kill him." He paused and swallowed noisily.

Lorne smiled and nodded, encouraging him to continue.

Another shuddering breath left his mouth, and tears began to fall. "Can you imagine what it must have been like to have witnessed your own father's death? Not only that but to see your own mother carry out the fateful deed. That image has haunted my days and nights for thirty-two years. I tremble when I'm in the same room as that woman, unsure whether I'll be next on her list. Lord knows I've certainly pissed her off enough over the years for her to want to punish me in the same kind of fashion."

Wanting to get to the crux of his painful story, Lorne urged, "What happened next, Joe? With the lamp?"

"It wasn't just any lamp. This was one of those oil lamps. The second she threw it, I squeezed my eyes shut. My father's screams forced them open again. Within seconds, he was engulfed in flames. His gaze latched on to mine as he reached for me. He mouthed three words, the only three words I ever wanted to hear from my mother, but never have: 'I love you.'" He broke down and buried his shaking head in his trembling hands.

Lorne sniffed and swiftly wiped away the tear that had escaped.

Sally looked dumbfounded by the man's account.

Swallowing down the lump that had formed in her throat, Lorne said, "My heart bleeds for you, Joe. To have witnessed such a dreadful incident at such a young age beggars belief. To have lived with that image through your childhood must have been traumatic for you. Did you receive any form of counselling?"

"Not in the respect you're talking about. My mother dished out her own futile attempt at counselling, which came in the form of threats. To be honest, I think she's possibly lived on her nerves for years since I left the family home."

"In case you blew the whistle on her?" Lorne queried.

"Yes. It's taken me most of my life to grow a backbone, to rise up against her."

Lorne was puzzled by his statement because it certainly hadn't seemed as though he'd rebelled in any way at the funeral, unless he was referring to arranging their meeting. "And will you, Joe? Rise up against her? What are your intentions?" she asked cautiously.

His gaze met hers, and his eyes narrowed for a split second before reverting to normal. "Nothing unlawful, if that's what you're asking, Inspector. I think it's time my mother paid for her actions."

"Are you saying that you'd be willing to work with us on bringing your mother to justice?"

He nodded and reached for his glass. "I am."

"I have to ask, why? Why now, Joe?"

"Because yet another innocent man has lost his life just because he is—or should I say *was*—associated with this family. Allan was extremely lucky to have escaped the family with his life, although my understanding is that he has grossly suffered financially in the process."

"Did he tell you that?" Lorne asked.

"No, we're not in contact with each other. I overheard my mother speaking with Teagan about the situation. Actually, that's an understatement—they were laughing about it."

"When was this?" Sally asked.

"After the divorce went through. I can't recall why there was a family gathering called, but that's when the conversation occurred. It seems that a big falling-out has taken place since then. Surely you saw the divide between them all at the funeral today?"

"We did notice, yes. What do you think is behind the split, Joe?" Lorne had her suspicions, but she wanted to see if Joe had come to the same conclusion. He shrugged and turned to look out the window again. Lorne grimaced. *Have I pushed him too far?* "Joe, please don't stop communicating with us now."

"I'm not. I'm mulling over what will happen once the truth comes out, *all* of it!"

"Joe, if you need protecting, we can arrange witness protection for you. It's not as if you will mind being cut off from your family like other people who have benefited from the scheme, is it?"

"Let me think about that for a few days, Inspector. This is a big deal for me."

"I appreciate that. I also understand how difficult it will be to destroy your family, which to be honest is likely to occur when you divulge any secrets they have."

Joe nodded again.

"The one thing I'll ask you to consider, Joe, is to always have your father's image in your mind. If nothing else, do it for him. Your mother betrayed him in the most damning way possible. Do not let her be allowed to continue to ruin people's lives. Is she behind Ryan's murder?"

He looked Lorne in the eye. "I believe so, in a roundabout way. I can't say anything else now, not until I've thoroughly considered my future."

Lorne's heart sank at the thought of him backing out. *Is he toying with me? Is he as bad, if not worse, than his family?* She wondered if he took some kind of warped pleasure in raising the hopes of coppers. Why hadn't he come forward earlier about his father's death? Maybe he had. When she got back to London, she could look into Joe's background, as well as the rest of the family's. These people *had* to be stopped, one way or another—of that much, she was certain. "If not your mother, are you telling us that maybe Lucy is involved in her husband's death?"

"Don't push me, Inspector. I've asked you to let me think over your proposal. If you're not willing to give me that time, then I'll have no other option than to walk away now."

Lorne saw Sally turn her way out of the corner of her eye, no doubt waiting to see her reaction to his threat. Lorne was seething— she was tempted to slap the cuffs on Joe, but she feared he would likely clam up altogether.

"We're willing to give you the time, Joe, especially as the recompense will be beneficial to us. How long are you staying in the area?"

"I'll be making my way home in the morning. I promise to call you once I've made my decision."

Lorne placed one of her business cards on the table in front of him. "Let's hope that call comes soon, Joe. I'd hate this family to get away with yet another murder."

Lorne and Sally finished their drinks and left the bar.

"Jesus! What a bloody tease! Do you think that was intentional, or do you genuinely think he had a change of heart halfway through the conversation?" Sally asked as they jumped in the car.

"I'm at a loss what to think, to be honest. If anything, it has made me even more determined to go after the matriarch of this twisted family. To me, it sounds as if she hates men and only uses them to obtain what she needs before discarding them."

"That's the conclusion I came to, as well. She likely gets bored with them and swiftly moves on to the next man—or victim," Sally agreed as they drove along the narrow country lane, heading towards her home.

"Exactly. I'm thinking along the lines of a black widow."

"Hmm… does this mean you'll be in need of a bed for an extra few days, Lorne?"

She turned to face her old friend. "Would you mind? It would be nice to catch up properly. I think we make a pretty hot team."

"What about the investigation back in London?"

"Katy can deal with things there. I think we should tear this family apart while we have them all in the same vicinity."

"One last question before we switch off our professional heads for the night. Do you think Lucy killed Ryan? She seemed so shocked when we shared the news of his death."

"I'm not sure, Sally. I don't know about you, but over the years, I've witnessed some incredible play-acting by supposedly grieving widows. I think it would be foolish not to keep her in our sights, for now at least. I hope I'm wrong, for her sake. However, I do believe that someone in that family is behind Ryan's death. We just need to find the evidence to back up my theory."

"As simple as that, eh?" Sally laughed.

CHAPTER EIGHTEEN

On the journey into the station the following morning, Lorne was deep in thought. She and Sally spent numerous hours the evening before going over all the details of the crime, and they'd toppled into bed feeling frustrated at one in the morning.

"Silly question, but what are you thinking about?" Sally asked as she waited for the lights to change at a junction.

"I'm thinking what the consequences would be of me hanging around here for the next few days. How do you think your chief is going to react? Should I get my chief to pave the way?"

"Okay, firstly, I think your involvement at this end is an outstanding idea. Secondly and thirdly, if I tell the chief you're needed, he should be able to accept my reasoning. However, a little nudge from your chief might be beneficial, too."

Lorne got out her mobile. "Good. I'll ring Katy first, make her aware of my plans. She's more than capable of running the team in my absence, and then I'll call Sean Roberts, my chief. He should be supportive to the idea; he usually is."

Katy had no objections to Lorne overseeing the investigation in Norfolk, especially as most, if not all, of the game players were in the area. Sean was a little more hesitant in his acceptance of the situation. Nevertheless, it didn't take Lorne long to make him see sense. He agreed to give her forty-eight hours to come up with the goods.

Sally and Lorne entered the station but parted at the top of the stairs. Sally insisted that Lorne make herself at home in her office while she dropped in on the chief. A large knot constricted Lorne's stomach as she awaited Sally's arrival.

Sally's face was darker than a storm cloud when she appeared in the doorway of her own office.

"Oh God, that bad, eh? Shall I get on the road now?"

Sally laughed. "No, I'm winding you up. I think we caught him on one of his good days; such a relief, as they tend to come around less frequently than a lunar eclipse."

"Fabulous news. What's first on the agenda?"

"Continue with the background checks, I suppose. Do you think we should prioritise Joe's first?"

"Why don't I do that? Maybe we can call him later this morning to see if he's changed his mind about the witness protection scheme."

"Good idea. I'm going to look into the Timcotts' finances, see what that throws up. Not before we've had a coffee, though."

Sally left the office and returned with two cups of coffee, which they drank while studying the files of all the family members once more.

After downing the last of her drink, Lorne asked, "Can I have access to a computer?"

"Come with me." Sally led Lorne to a desk that held a computer monitor and keyboard. "You might get a little hot here. It's right next to the radiator."

Lorne smiled. "Suits me. I tend to feel the cold more than most folks anyway. I'll let you know if I find anything significant."

"Ditto."

A few hours into the research, Lorne sat back in her chair and tapped her pen on her chin. Nothing constructive had surfaced in Joe's background. As far as Lorne could tell, throughout his life, all thirty-seven years of it, he'd avoided any form of trouble. Deep in thought, she jolted when her mobile rang. "Hi, Katy. How's it going?"

"Are you sitting down, Lorne?"

She sat upright in her chair and sought out a blank piece of paper on which to take notes. "That sounds ominous. Hit me with it."

"Right, I have to say I never saw this coming, and it's going to blow your bloody socks off."

"All right, girl. Get on with it!" Seeing Sally come out of her office, Lorne clicked her fingers and motioned for Sally to join her. "I'm going to put you on speaker. Sally's here with me."

Katy exhaled a large sigh before she spoke, and Lorne wondered if her partner was about to object to Sally's inclusion in the conversation, but Katy continued. "Crap, I genuinely don't know where to start. Only to say that I think we've messed up big time."

Lorne frowned. "Messed up? How? The investigation has hardly begun, Katy. We can only deal with the evidence as it comes in."

"That's just it—I'm not talking about Ryan Timcott's case, Lorne. It's the other case I'm referring to, that of Daniel Grade. I've just received the DNA results back… the results came back with a mind-blowing revelation. Forensics found traces of saliva on the skin of Grade's penis."

Lorne cringed then laughed at Sally's wide-eyed expression. "You're going to tell me he had a blowjob before someone cut his dick off, right?"

"Yep, but this is the incredible part—the results match the DNA of someone on our database—a well-known drug addict in the area who has been arrested for dealing and other petty theft crimes."

"I have a pen poised, waiting for that person's name."

"It's Olga Smitz," Katy stated before falling silent.

Lorne contemplated the name for a moment or two. It sounded familiar, and she dug into her memory bank to obtain the answer.

"Are you still there, Lorne?" Katy asked, amusement in her tone.

"I'm here. I recognise the name, but I can't recall where from, Katy. Help me out please?"

"Olga Smitz, youngest daughter of…"

"Bloody hell! Claire Knight. Jesus!" Goose bumps broke out on Lorne's skin. In spite of the heat hitting her from the radiator, ice blocks had filled her veins.

"Precisely. The cases are linked," Katy said.

"I don't understand, hon. How have we messed up?" Lorne asked, shuddering away the chill encompassing her.

"*I've* messed up, not *we*. The phone Olga used to call his wife. I put the information to one side and forgot all about it. I'm blaming that on my forgetfulness due to this damn pregnancy."

"You can pack that in, for a start. Shit happens, Katy. There's no real damage done. It's only been a few days since the incident occurred. Don't beat yourself up about it."

"What shall we do? Arrest her?" Katy asked.

Lorne looked up at Sally. "Shall we? There's a possibility we could stir up a bucket-load of shit if we turn up at Lucy's house right now."

Sally nodded thoughtfully. "We have to, Lorne. We can't afford to let Olga leave the area. We might never find her again. I'll arrange a couple of PCs to join us, just in case we hit any trouble." Sally marched into her office.

"Are you all right, Katy?"

Her partner sighed. "Yeah, majorly pissed off. Feel as though I've let you down."

"Don't! You haven't, and we'll have it sorted, hopefully before the day is out. Can you e-mail me the evidence? We'll pick her up and drag her in for questioning."

"Sure. I'll do it right away. Good luck with the arrest. Let me know what happens later if you can."

"Gotcha. Take care."

Lorne disconnected the call and sat back in her chair, resisting the urge to rub her hands together like an excited teenager.

Sally stormed out of her office, her coat on, ready to get going. "Are you fit?"

Lorne picked up her thick jacket and followed Sally out of the incident room, sweeping past the rest of the team, who were issuing their encouragement.

The two police cars—one marked, the other belonging to Sally—pulled into the drive of Lucy Timcott's home at eleven forty-five. "Looks like no one has left yet," Lorne stated, guessing by the number of vehicles parked in the drive.

Once all four coppers were out of their cars and standing on the front doorstep of the mansion, Sally gave a rallying call. "Let's hit them hard and fast." She rang the bell.

The Thai housekeeper opened the door. Sally and Lorne flashed their badges and barged into the house. "Where are they?" Lorne demanded.

The woman pointed a shaking finger in the direction of the living room where she and Sally had visited Lucy the previous week. Sally opened the door, and Lorne stood alongside her. The two uniformed officers stood menacingly behind them.

"Inspectors? What are you doing here?" Lucy asked, appearing puzzled. "Have you come to tell me you've found out who killed my husband?" Lucy sank back in her chair as if uttering the words had sapped all her strength.

"We're getting there, Lucy. Is your sister Olga around?" Sally asked.

"She's upstairs, sleeping. What do you want with her?"

Lorne's gaze locked with Claire's and held it for a few moments before the mother glanced at Lucy.

Sally motioned for the officers to stand near the bottom of the stairs. "We'd like a chat with her. All right if I go upstairs?"

"I don't understand. Why do you want to talk to Olga? Is this about Ryan's death?"

"Not exactly. We'd rather not go into detail until we've spoken to your sister," Sally replied, then spun on her heel and led the officers up the stairs.

Lorne had decided in the car that Sally should make the arrest, while she remained with the other family members to gauge their reaction as the events unfolded.

Lucy appeared confused and asked her mother, "What do you think this is about, Mum? Has Olga done something wrong?"

Claire shrugged. "I have no idea what that child gets up to. Maybe it's to do with her habit. I've warned her countless times not to be reliant on the damn drugs. Does she listen to me? No! Is that what this is about, Inspector?"

Before Lorne could reply, a commotion broke out upstairs. Olga started shouting and cursing. It sounded like a herd of buffalo thundering across the floor above.

"Ouch, you'll pay for that," one of the male officers shouted.

A psychotic laugh travelled down the stairs and into the living room.

Claire left her seat and walked into the hallway. "Don't fight them, Olga. I'll get onto the solicitor now."

"Wise words, Mrs. Knight. You can tell your solicitor to show up at the police station in Wymondham. That's where your daughter is going to be held for questioning."

"On what charge, Inspector?"

"Murder!"

Lucy bounced forward in her chair. "You're making a mistake. Olga would never do such a thing." She gasped as if something had just dawned on her. "You don't mean *she's* the one who killed Ryan, do you?"

"There's every possibility. At the moment, we're taking her in for questioning about another crime, unrelated to Ryan's death. Let's leave it at that for now. Your husband's case is ongoing. New leads are coming our way every day." Lorne looked over at Claire, who was studying her through dark eyes filled with hatred. "It's only a matter of time before we begin to slot all the pieces of this puzzle together, Lucy. We should have a definitive answer for you shortly. After all, there are two experienced police forces working the case."

"But Olga wouldn't hurt a fly. I know her," Lucy appealed.

"Hush, child. Don't say another word. Leave the solicitor to wipe the floor with these insufferable people who have nothing better to do all day than sit behind their desks, surmising they know who the criminals are, only to be wrong half the time."

"And you're talking from experience there, are you, Mrs. Knight?"

Claire harrumphed and folded her arms in defiance. More shouting from upstairs was followed by several pairs of feet stomping down the stairs as Olga continued to fight and shout at the arresting officers. Lorne walked into the hallway to find the woman standing there half-naked with a uniformed officer holding onto an arm on either side.

"You can't take my daughter dressed like *that*. I won't allow it!" Claire bellowed, her cheeks flushed with anger.

Sally smiled at Claire. "We gave her the option of getting dressed, but she chose that opportunity to lash out at Rob over here." Sally pointed to the young officer sporting a bruise on his left eye, wincing in pain. "We'll hit her with an assaulting a police officer and a resisting arrest charge on top of the murder charge."

Olga immediately stopped wriggling, and her mouth dropped open. She turned to look at her mother, pleading swimming in her eyes.

Claire turned her back on her child and returned to the living room.

"Take her out to the car. Pick up her coat on the way out, boys," Sally ordered as the constables tightened their grip on the suspect and left the house.

Joining Lorne, Lucy, and Claire in the living room, Sally gave Claire a business card. "Olga will be residing with us for the next few days at this address."

Claire snatched the card from Sally's hand. "I beg to differ. My solicitor will get her out of there before the end of the day. Mark my words on that."

Lorne looked over at Lucy, who still seemed shell-shocked. She had a cigarette burning down to the stub in her left hand, forgotten about during the fracas. Lorne rescued the butt before the ash dropped on the deep-piled beige carpet. "Are you all right, Lucy?" she whispered, crouching before her.

Lucy's eyes glazed over, and she shook her head. "Truthfully, I don't know."

"Leave her alone. I'll see to my daughter when you've gone."

Lorne's eyes narrowed when she glanced Claire's way. She spoke again to Lucy. "Do you want to speak to us without your mother being present?"

"No, she does not! Get out!" Claire shouted, launching herself at Lorne.

Sally quickly intervened before Claire got halfway across the room. "I wouldn't do that, not unless you want an assaulting a police officer lying at your door, too, Claire."

"Tell her to leave my daughter alone then, and I'll back off."

"Why?" Sally asked. "What are you afraid Lucy will tell us?"

"Don't be absurd." Claire threw her arms up in the air and paced the floor. "This is nothing but police harassment. Stop *harassing* my daughter, forcing her to say something she doesn't want to tell you."

"Do you see any harassment going on, Lucy?" Lorne gently asked the confused young woman.

Lucy shook her head. "No."

"Sally, why don't you take Claire outside? The fresh air might help her to calm down."

"Good idea. Come with me, Mrs. Knight." Sally held Claire by the elbow and escorted her out into the garden. The woman appeared to apply her brakes and dug her heels into the carpet.

Once the patio door shut behind her colleague, Lorne asked Lucy, "Is there something you want to get off your chest?"

Lucy's eyes welled up with tears. "No. I just want all this aggro to stop so that I can get on with my grieving. Do you have any news on what happened to Ryan yet, Inspector? It's the not knowing that is tearing me apart."

"I can understand that, Lucy, and no, we're no further forward with our investigation. We do have a few leads that we hope to chase up in the next few days. However, your sister's arrest was propelled to the top of our agenda once the DNA evidence came through on another murder. Has she said anything to you about the incident?"

Lucy's hand clutched at her chest. "No, this is the first I've heard about it. Who has she killed? For what reason? Do you know?"

"A man called Daniel Grade. Have you heard of him? He's a bank manager in the Fulham area."

"No, I've never heard his name mentioned. Is there a link between his death and Ryan's, do you think?"

"What makes you say that, Lucy?"

She hitched up a shoulder. "I don't know, because they were in the same line of business, I suppose. Financial services."

"It's certainly a line of enquiry we'll be going down. Do you think Ryan might have known the man? Is there any way you can find out for us, perhaps through your husband's address book?"

"I can have a look and get back to you later. I want to go out today for some bits and bobs, and to escape Mum's suffocation. I could call into the office and have a snoop around. Inspector, what my sister has done is appalling, but please, don't tar us all with the same brush."

What a strange thing to say! Lorne decided not to challenge Lucy about her statement. At that moment, she needed the woman to obtain the information about a possible connection between Ryan and Daniel Grade. Then she would revisit Lucy's plea at a later date.

"We'll look forward to receiving your call. You can contact Sally at the Wymondham station. I'm sorry your mother is giving you a hard time. That's not acceptable when you're trying to deal with your grief. Has she always been an unsympathetic type of person? Your brother intimated the same thing when we spoke to him at the funeral." Lorne felt if she mentioned Joe briefly at this point, it would encourage Lucy to open up more.

"Joe? You've spoken to Joe? I miss Joe. He fell out of love with us all when he left the family home years ago, and yes, mother doesn't tend to possess a sympathetic bone in her body. You get used to it, Inspector."

"That's a shame, on both counts." Lorne looked over her shoulder to see if the door to the garden was still closed. She whispered, "I want to ask you if you think either Olga or your other sisters, or your mother even, could be involved in your husband's murder?"

"The truth is, I just don't know anymore. For instance, I would never have dreamed that Olga was capable of murdering someone. Saying that, I don't know if that's a one-off due to her drug habit. Could it be?"

"That is a possibility. However, I still have your brother's words ringing in my ears."

"Joe is such a sensitive soul. We used to be so similar. I kind of came out of my shell when I met Ryan. I loved him so much. He gave me the strength to stand up to my mother, if only a little."

"Did Ryan have any business dealings with your mother?" Lucy's reluctance to respond immediately raised a red flag to Lorne. "Lucy?"

"Yes. They always seemed to have secrets between them. I can't tell you the amount of times I've walked into the room and witnessed the conversation instantly dry up. It used to really annoy me. Every time I challenged Ryan about it, he waved away my fears as though I was being childish and reading things into it that just weren't there."

"Are you saying that he didn't trust you, Lucy?"

"I guess I am. That hurt. It did when he was alive and even more so now he's gone. Perhaps if he had trusted me, he might still be alive today. What I struggle to comprehend is why he trusted my mother."

"Well, the more we're learning about your mother, I sense she probably had some kind of hold over him."

"I don't understand."

Lorne smiled weakly. "Maybe she was able to blackmail him in some way."

Lucy gasped. Just then, Claire barged into the room, and it all kicked off again. Lorne rose to her feet and placed her hands in front of her. "Calm down, Claire. Can't you see how much your anger is upsetting your daughter?"

"That's ridiculous. Your intrusion into her house and carting her sister off under false pretences has done that."

Lorne looked past Claire at Sally. "Are we ready to go?"

"I think so. The quicker we get Olga back to the station and start interviewing her, the better."

"Not before our solicitor arrives," Claire stated with a venomous tongue.

Lorne's eyes rolled up to the ceiling. *Change your tune, woman, for goodness' sake.*

CHAPTER NINETEEN

During the ride back to the station, Lorne and Sally took the time to discuss the tactics they would use to question Olga, who was travelling in the back of the other police car with the two constables.

Lorne shuddered. "Why do I sense that won't be the last time we lay eyes on Claire today?"

"You think? She was bloody furious when I was out in the garden with her. I had to block her path more than once. She kept trying to look over my shoulder to see what you were getting up to with her daughter."

"She's trouble with a capital T, that one. After chatting to both Joe and Lucy, I think her children have had a hell of a lot to contend with throughout their lives. I got the impression they are all frightened of her. That reminds me, I'm going to give Joe a ring at the hotel, see if he's changed his mind."

"Good idea. It would be great to have something concrete to hand when we go after the indomitable Claire Knight."

Lorne dialled the hotel's number. "Hello there. This is DI Lorne Warner. I was wondering if you could put me through to Joe Knight's room please?"

"Ahh, I'm sorry. He checked out a few moments ago. If you hold on a second, I'll see if he's still in the car park."

"That'd be great, thanks." Lorne tutted. "Damn, looks like he's gone," she told Sally.

"Hello? I'm sorry. His car is no longer in the car park. I can give you his contact number if you like?"

"That would be great." Lorne jotted down Joe's mobile number and ended the call. She immediately tried to get in touch with him. The phone rang and rang before Joe finally answered.

"Hello, Joe?"

"Yes, who is this?"

"Joe, it's DI Warner. We met at your hotel last night."

"Yes, of course. Please don't start pestering me every five minutes, Inspector. I asked you to give me time to think things over."

"I'm not trying to put pressure on you, Joe, I promise. I'm ringing up to make you aware of an arrest we've just made."

"An arrest? Who?"

"One of your sisters. It's in connection with a murder that took place last week back in London."

"My God! Which one?"

"Olga. We're taking her back to the station now for questioning. I was ringing to tell you the news, hoping that it might prompt you into making the right decision." Silence filled the line. "Joe? Are you still there?"

"Yes, I'm here. Olga, that's incredible. I would never have believed it of her. I suppose it was only a matter of time before mother got her claws into her. How awful. I'm at a loss what to say, Inspector."

"I'm sorry this has come as a big shock to you, Joe. Surely you can see the seriousness of the situation and how much the information you can tell us regarding your family can help? With your help, we could get them off the street and in prison. The murders are stacking up, and so are the suspects. So far, they're all linked to your family. And then there's your father's death to consider, of course."

"I'm tempted, Inspector. They're all evil, every last one of them."

"Are you including Lucy in that sweeping statement, too?"

"She's had her moments over the years. She might come across as an innocent bystander to you, but I can assure you she isn't. Whatever she's told you in the last few days, that'll be her grief forming the words."

"Then help us. They're crafty. They've spent years covering their tracks as far as we can tell. You know that. Your input could nail them once and for all."

"I thought you understood my dilemma, Inspector. You said you were willing to give me time. Now, I just feel as though you're forcing me to help you lock my family up."

"I'm sorry if that's how it's coming across, Joe. All I'm doing is trying to be truthful with you."

"I'll do a deal with you."

Lorne inhaled a large breath in anticipation. "I'm listening."

"You're questioning Olga, right? Let's see what she can tell you first. You'll have to push her hard to get the answers, though, I assure you. From what I overheard during the funeral, that one is up to her eyes in mischief."

Lorne clenched her fist and hit the dashboard. Sally patted her thigh and made a 'calm down' motion with her hand as she drove. "Okay, will it be all right to ring you later on today?"

"Make it tomorrow instead. I think you'll be indisposed with my sister for many hours to come. She's always been fond of passing the buck when in the shit."

"And if she dishes the dirt, will you back up her story? The more people who report the accuracies to her statement, the better the judgement will be."

"I'll consider it. If it was left up to me, I would rather stand back and let them dig their own graves. I have enough guilt rattling around inside because of the way my father died as it is. Have you any idea how heavy that particular burden is to carry around all these years?"

"I can imagine, Joe. But I'm also aware that other people carrying such traumatic burdens have felt a huge sense of liberation once they have righted a large wrong. That could be your situation, if you confide in us."

"Years of therapy haven't helped rid me of the guilt, Inspector. Therefore, I doubt what you're saying is true. Give me a ring tomorrow."

Lorne held the phone away from her ear. She hit the end call button and threw her mobile into her lap. "He hung up on me. Damn, I hope I haven't damaged the good relationship we had with him."

"You're reading too much into it, Lorne. The news probably came as a shock to him, caught him off balance for a second or two. We've got Olga in our grasp. Let's make sure we use every trick available to worm the information out of her. Hey, she might even surprise us and reveal *all* the family's grim, dark secrets. You can't tell with druggies which way the pendulum is going to swing."

"Have you had many dealings with druggies in the past in the depths of Norfolk, Sally?"

"Once or twice. You just need to have your wits about you and strike when they're at their most vulnerable."

Lorne laughed. "Let's hope that feat doesn't take us all night to accomplish."

They pulled into the car park and helped Olga, who was wrapped in a blanket, out of the back of the police car and hurried her inside the station, out of the chilling wind cutting across the open area. Sally instructed the duty sergeant to book Olga into a cell and supply her with suitable clothing then asked him to call them once the suspect's solicitor arrived for the interview.

Olga remained silent, staring at the floor, during the proceedings as if contemplating how much trouble she was in.

Lorne and Sally walked up the stairs to the incident room. Lorne removed her jacket, and after grabbing a coffee from the machine, she rang Katy to bring her up to date.

"That's excellent news. Do you think Olga is behind Ryan's death, too?"

"I'm not sure at this point. Is everything all right there?"

"Plodding on. I've decided to see what I can find out about Claire Knight's second husband. It bothers me that she appears to have talked her way out of two very serious crimes, in spite of her being present at the scene. Are we looking at a case of police incompetence or her ability to play the grieving widow with great poise? Either way, I intend to find out the whys and wherefores. I know one thing—neither you nor I would have let her get away with it."

"Ain't that the truth? Check into her solicitors' background, too, will you, Katy? Both past and present. That might be the key as to why she got let off scot-free."

"Will do. Have you rung Tony?"

"No, is there a problem at home?"

"Chill! No, I just wondered. I know how much you guys pine for each other when you're apart," Katy teased.

"That's bullshit!" Lorne chuckled, but Katy was right—she was missing Tony, a lot. "I'm going to get my Tony fix now via the phone."

"Say hi from me. Will you ring me later, after you've questioned Olga?"

"Of course. I think we're in for a long day, so I'll probably get back to you tomorrow, all right?"

"Enjoy! Rip her apart, Lorne." Katy ended the call with a growl.

Lorne disconnected the call and rang home, only to find that everything was fine and that Charlie was getting ready for another hot date with Brandon at the agility club.

"You look contemplative. Is Tony missing you?" Sally asked, perching on the edge of her borrowed desk.

"He's fine. I think I'm losing my daughter, though."

"How come? Is she moving out? Doesn't she run the kennels for you?"

"Gosh, bombard me with questions, why don't you? It's hard being a mother and seeing your daughter embroiled in a life that doesn't involve you. She's spending more and more time with this new fella of hers, and…" Lorne waved her hand in front of her. "Don't listen to me. I talk a lot of crap at times. Any news on the brief yet?"

"Yep, he's just arrived, along with an unexpected guest."

Lorne frowned. "Guest? Who's that?"

"Olga's mother, the infamous Mrs. Butter-Wouldn't-Melt Knight."

Shaking her head, Lorne smiled. "Looks like she's in for a long wait, then, doesn't it?"

"That's bound to piss her off even more than she was back at the house."

"It'll be interesting to see how she reacts. Maybe we'll be able to arrest her for assaulting a police officer. It would be nice to have something over her for a change. She makes my ruddy skin crawl with her 'I'm so much better than you lot put together' bloody attitude."

Sally laughed. "She's really got under your skin."

"Yeah, and that's the sodding thing that bugs me most about her. I've dealt with some vicious frigging criminals over the years who have never had the upper hand, but her? Well, at the moment, I'll give her that one in the hope that we'll soon be able to wipe the smug grin off her face, once we have the facts to hand."

"Just don't let her see how much she's getting to you, Lorne," Sally advised.

Lorne winked. "That's my intention. Now, with her daughter Olga, that's going to be a totally different story. She's going to wish she never sucked on that poor man's dick, let alone cut it off and shoved it in his mouth like a lollipop."

Sally's hand covered her mouth as a giggle broke out. "Let's get this action rolling."

Lorne and Sally collected the solicitor from the reception area. Knight shot daggers at each of them as she rose from her seat.

Sally shook her head and waved a finger. "You're not going anywhere, Mrs. Knight. You have no right to be involved in this process. In fact, we could be hours, so I really don't think it would be wise for you to hang around here awaiting your daughter's release."

"Can you stop me sitting here?" Claire said through gritted teeth.

Sally heaved out an exaggerated sigh. "No, we can't stop you hanging around here. I hope you have a very strong resolve, however, because the odd tramp shows up wanting a warm in reception occasionally."

"If that's supposed to scare me off, you've failed. I'll be here for the duration."

"That's your prerogative. You won't be given any special treatment. As long as we're clear on that from the outset, then please, make yourself comfortable."

Claire sneered at Sally and Lorne. She turned to her male solicitor and patted him on the back. "Go do your best for my baby, Ken. There's a bonus in it for you if you successfully get Olga out of here this evening."

The dressed-to-impress solicitor smiled at Claire and nodded. "I'll do my very best, as always."

Lorne stepped aside so that Sally and the solicitor, Ken Wallace, could walk up the hallway to the interview room ahead of her. The three of them entered and sat in silence around the table in the stark white room, waiting for the suspect. A female PC opened the door, pulled a reluctant handcuffed Olga into the room, and settled her in the chair next to the solicitor.

After saying the required information for the recording machine, Sally hit Olga with the first question. "Olga, where and when did you meet Daniel Grade?"

Olga turned slightly to look at her brief before uttering the words Lorne had prepared herself to hear. "No comment." The interview continued back and forth for the next few hours. Sally asked the same questions over and over, until finally, Olga snapped, "I've told you—no bloody comment. Change the record, for God's sake."

"I'll change the questions if you agree to give us your full cooperation. At present, the only person you're successfully pissing off is your mother. Is that your intention, Olga?"

The woman's nose screwed up in confusion. "What the fuck are you talking about?"

"She's outside waiting for you. Has been for hours. Until now, your lack of cooperation has done nothing for your mother's anger management issues," Sally said, issuing the solicitor with a smile.

"Totally uncalled-for comment, Inspector. You'd be advised to stick to questioning my client."

"Is it, Mr. Wallace? From what we've learned recently about Olga's mother, I'd say she rules this family like some kind of dictator."

Lorne almost choked on the laugh stuck in her throat.

Wallace shared a warning glance with his client. Olga shrugged and looked down at her clenched hands.

"Anything to say about that description, Olga? Is DI Parker accurate in her perception?" Lorne prompted when no one chose to speak.

"What am I supposed to say? You obviously know her well enough to make that assumption."

"Olga!" Wallace warned out of the corner of his mouth.

"Let her speak, Mr. Wallace. We're keen to hear what your client has to say about her darling mother," Lorne snapped at him.

Olga chortled. "Never heard those two words in the same sentence before, 'darling mother.' Truth be told, some of us girls have had enough. We're rising up against her. Teagan thinks she's past it."

"And was it Teagan who instructed you to kill Daniel Grade?" Sally asked.

Olga fell silent. After a few moments thinking, she replied, "Yes. I swear, I've never done anything like this before. Fifty grand proved to be too much of a temptation for me in the end."

Wallace stared open-mouthed at his client, which amused Lorne immensely. *Apparently you don't know the depths this family will go to for money, after all, matey.*

"So you were given specific instructions to kill Grade. Is that what you're telling us?" Lorne pushed.

"Yes."

"For what reason?" Sally enquired.

Olga shrugged. "Teagan told me to get the money and papers from him then finish him off."

"What papers?" Lorne asked, enjoying the way the interview was panning out with both she and Sally asking alternating questions as if they could read each other's mind.

"How the hell should I know? I wasn't interested. All I was worried about was getting my hands on that fifty K."

"And what did you use the money for, Olga? I'm taking a wild guess here and saying it was to feed your habit. Am I right?"

Olga exhaled a large breath. "Yeah, you're right. Although I told Teagan I was going to buy myself a spell in rehab with the funds. She was that thrilled, she pushed her usual partner in crime aside and gave me the job."

"And who usually carries out Teagan's instructions? Would that be Helen?"

"Yes. Those two are inseparable."

Wallace cleared his throat and interjected. "Olga, I must warn you only to answer the questions that are directed at you personally."

"Nonsense, Mr. Wallace. Your client has the right to speak openly during this interview. If she wants to get other things off her chest regarding her siblings and mother during this time, then she has the right to do just that," Sally chastised him.

He grunted and looked down at his legal pad once more.

"You were saying, Olga? Teagan and Helen are inseparable. Does that mean they often carry out crimes as a twosome?" Lorne smiled at the young woman.

"Mostly, yes."

Lorne nodded. "Would that include killing your brother-in-law Ryan, for instance?"

Olga chewed on her lip—a telling sign to an interrogating officer. Lorne pressed her for an answer. "Does that mean yes?"

Olga gave her brief a sideways glance and nodded.

"Sorry, nodding is not acceptable. You need to speak your response for the tape."

"Yes."

"I want this interview stopped so I can instruct my client," Wallace demanded, his rage showing as his pad hit the desk.

"That's not going to happen, Mr. Wallace."

He glared at Lorne. "I'm going to take this higher, make a formal complaint."

"That's your entitlement," Sally assured him. "Olga, are you telling us that Teagan and Helen were the two women aboard the boat with your brother-in-law before it exploded?"

"Yes, they told me they did it. Lucy has no idea, though."

"Interesting. How about your mother? Where does she fit into all of this?"

Wallace slammed his notebook on the desk again, scaring Lorne. "I must insist you retract that question immediately."

Lorne's brow furrowed. "Can I ask why, Mr. Wallace? It seems a pretty legitimate question to be asking."

"I've told you before, this interview should concern what my client knows about the incident you have arrested her for, nothing else."

His outburst made Lorne turn to Sally whose puzzled look mirrored her own feelings. "Is there anything in the rule book about other topics not being allowed to be raised during an interview, Inspector? If there is I must have missed that particular part."

Lorne shook her head. "I don't seem to recall that particular rule."

"This is bullshit. You two are wind-up merchants, not like any investigating officers I've ever dealt with in the past."

"And there we have it, Mr. Wallace. DI Warner and I have successfully hit a trail leading to this family's door, and it's ablaze with guilt. Previous coppers may not have seen the signs pointing in their direction, but we're better than any of our colleagues. We dig deeper and scrutinise all the evidence until something floats to the surface and sparks our interest. That's how we caught your client in the first place. One teeny-weeny drop of saliva on a man's penis, and bingo bango! There's no getting away from placing your client at the scene. The question running through my mind is why previous colleagues have pushed aside valuable clues and evidence as it showed up?" Sally stopped to let the words sink in to both the brief and his client. She turned to Lorne and raised an eyebrow to finish her conclusion.

"I'm thinking that money talks, Inspector Parker. Isn't that right, Mr. Wallace? You've been with this family for—what? Around fifteen years? In that time, how often have you crossed the sweaty palms of officers in the hope they will look elsewhere for clues? Is that why the matriarch of this family got away with killing two of her husbands? Forgive me if I'm wrong, but that's what it looks like from where I'm sitting. There's no other explanation for it."

Wallace sneered first at his client and then at Lorne and Sally. "Ludicrous, pure conjecture for which you have no evidence. If you think I'm going to admit to anything, you'll have a very long wait. My loyalty to this family, and Claire Knight in particular, will never be tested, not by you or anyone else in the legal system. That includes judges."

"What an interesting outburst." Lorne smiled one of her killer smiles, aware she had him pinned into a corner. "So, by that statement, we're to assume that you have several judges on the payroll, too. Please tell me I've misread your meaning?"

Wallace blustered and picked up his notebook once again. "This interview is in connection with my client, not me. Please continue, with caution, *detectives.*"

Lorne chuckled internally as the redness in his cheeks rose to a dangerous level and his finger ran along the edge of his shirt collar. "Are you happy to continue, Olga?"

"Yes."

"Do you get on with your brother, Joe?" Sally asked.

"Not really. I used to, but not now. He chickened out, left the family home when I was quite young. I saw that as detrimental to our family."

"May I ask why?" asked Lorne.

"Because he's a man. We've never had what I call a 'great male role model' in the family. Joe should have stuck around. Maybe things would have been different if he had."

"Different? Are you referring to your drug habit?" Sally probed.

Olga nodded. "Yes."

"And you think having a male presence, one that you could rely on; living in the family home, would have taken your life on a different journey?"

"I believe so. I didn't want to get involved in drugs. Some people turn to drink for a cry for help; I turned to drugs instead."

"How does your mother feel about your drug habit, Olga?"

"She abhors it. Sometimes, I think she abhors me more."

"Are you telling us that your cries for help went unnoticed by the one person you needed to help you most?" Sally queried.

"I suppose so. All of us, all we ever wanted was to make Mum love us. She's cold and unfeeling."

"Why did your mother have so many children if she lacks maternal instincts?" Lorne asked quietly.

Olga's head dropped onto her chest. "I don't know. I guess you should ask her that."

"So, is that why your family turned to crime? In order to gain attention—her attention? You thought that would ultimately obtain the love you were desperately seeking, is that it?"

"Probably. She's always told us what to wear, what to do with our money—when we had any—and how to act when we're around certain people, mostly men with money."

Lorne glanced at the seething Wallace, who was frantically scribbling in his notebook, and wondered if he would have the balls to relay all this information back to Claire or whether he would just sit on the facts out of fear. "And that's the people your family mostly target? People with money to their names?"

"Yes, that and…" She appeared to reproach herself at that point.

Lorne filled in the gaps for her. "And those who have *access* to money?"

Olga nodded. "Going back to your role in the murder of Daniel Grade, did you see any of the papers you obtained from him?"

"No. I bought some dope on the way home with the money I took from him. Teagan was livid when she heard about what I'd done."

"Did your sister let on what sort of papers they were?" Lorne pressed.

"Sorry, no. Only that they were important ones."

"So these papers, are they part of a bigger picture, Olga?" Lorne asked.

"I don't know. Teagan put them in the safe as soon as I gave them to her. Once she shut the safe, she rubbed her hands together in glee. I was too far out of it to ask what they meant to her."

"The safe? Where is this safe?"

"At Teagan's house, although Mother has one, too. Actually, I think she has a couple of them."

"How did you feel when your mother *stole* the house from Allan?"

Wallace tutted and leaned over to whisper in his client's ear. Olga refused to answer the question.

However, Lorne was determined to get an answer. "Did you think it's right to rob a man of his lifetime's achievements? Have you seen where he's being forced to live now?"

"No. I never thought Mum was in the right on that score. Allan always treated her fairly, and yet she couldn't wait to get rid of him."

"Why? Did he outlive his usefulness, financially?"

"I don't know the ins and outs of their divorce. He can tell you more about that side of things than I can." Olga pointed a thumb in her brief's direction.

"Mr. Wallace, care to enlighten us about that?"

"No comment," he sneered. "This interview keeps wavering off topic, and I have no intention of answering any such questions, Inspectors. So kindly refrain from asking them "

"After speaking with Allan a few days ago, I have a rough idea of just what that marriage consisted of predominantly him giving and Claire taking. Does that sound about right, Olga?" Lorne asked.

Olga nodded. "Mum was running short of cash leading up to the time he walked into her life, wasn't she, Wallace?"

The brief neither responded nor looked up, just kept his gaze glued to his notebook.

"Well, it's true," Olga added in a huff.

There was a knock on the door, and a constable entered the room. Sally paused the recording as the PC handed Lorne a slip of paper. Sally looked over her shoulder and nudged her leg under the table. "You go. I'll finish questioning Olga," Sally urged.

Lorne smiled appreciatively and left the room. When she walked into the reception area, she found a nervous-looking Joe waiting for her. She shook his hand. "Hi, Joe. Give me two minutes to sort out a room." She approached the duty sergeant. "Is there a spare interview room I can use?" Leaning in closer, she asked, "Where's Mrs. Knight?"

Lowering his voice, the sergeant replied, "She left about fifteen minutes ago, fury guiding her exit," he added with a smile. "Room Three is vacant. Do you want me to organise a PC to sit in with you, ma'am?"

"No, I don't think that will be necessary. Did he bump into Mrs. Knight or not?"

"He came through the door a few minutes after she left. He looks worried. Are you sure you don't want company in there?"

Lorne waved away the suggestion. "He'll be fine once we're alone, I'm sure. Is the room open? Can I have some paper for notes?"

"The room's open. Here's the paper. I'll get someone to bring you both a coffee, if you like?"

"That's kind. Thanks." Lorne asked Joe to follow her, and they settled in the seats behind the desk in the small interview room. She placed the sheets of paper with a pen on top in front of her and folded her arms. "Are you aware that your mother was here just before you arrived?"

"I saw her get in a taxi before I made my move. She didn't look happy, Inspector."

"It's Lorne. No, I don't think she bargained on Olga's interview taking so long."

"Am I allowed to ask how it's going with Olga?"

"You are. She's cooperating with us, slowly but surely, giving us useful information. Much to her solicitor's disgust, I hasten to add," she told him, amusement running through her voice.

"I bet. He's been Mother's advisor for years. Another one not to be trusted. His opinions are easily bought. How is Olga holding up?"

"She's fine. We're not going to be hard on her as long as she keeps sharing information with us. I think my 'partner' will be going along the lines of a deal, a lesser charge, if she really comes up with a prime piece of information that will enable us to finally arrest your mother. I'm just trying to reassure you that what you and Olga can tell us could eventually end your mother's reign of terror. Surely that's got to be an incentive to help us, Joe?"

"It is, Insp... Lorne. I've thought long and hard about your proposal, and I'm willing to go ahead with the witness protection scheme."

"Okay, although I have to say, to be honest, I doubt you'll need it from what Olga is telling us in there."

"Ah, but Olga doesn't know everything. I do, at least up until the time I left the family home, in disgust."

"Well, hopefully, Olga can fill in the blanks from that time. Either way, I appreciate you coming in today. I'm not going to record our little chat, but I will be making notes, all right?"

"Of course. Where do you want me to begin?"

"You told us about how your father died. I'm aware of just how young you were back then, but can you tell me how your mother appeared to get away with a murder charge? By that I mean, how did the pair of you get out of the house, and what happened next?"

His hands clenched in front of him and twisted slightly as his knuckles turned white.

"Take your time, Joe."

"From what I can remember, I think Mother realised she'd gone too far. I could see the panic in her eyes. She tried to reach my father—maybe to help him, I don't know—but the flames by then had engulfed his body. She saw me sitting on the stairs and screeched at me to join her. Mother held out her hand and forced me to run past his burning body. She didn't even have the courage to come and collect me. Together, we escaped the house. The second we were outside, she started to scream for help. A couple of neighbours ran to our assistance. Bill from next door called for the fire brigade and the police. We lived in a semi. He probably only rang out of duty and to help save his own precious home from going up in flames. He always kept his distance from us."

"So once the police and the fire brigade arrived at the scene, did they get the fire under control easily, or did it take a huge effort on their part?"

"Once they'd set up, I think it only took a few moments to put the fire out."

"Did you hear your mother's explanation about how the fire started?"

"No, she told the police she was too traumatised to speak. We both spent the night in hospital. They sedated us, or me, because I was inconsolable. I think Mother saw my being upset and the attention I was receiving as a chance to get attention for herself. They gave her a stage, and she enjoyed her acting debut that night, if I'm not mistaken. That makes me sound such a callous bastard, I know, but that woman deliberately killed my father and revelled in the fact that people were taking genuine interest in her for a change. That's my perception of events, of course. I only came to that conclusion years later."

"What I don't understand is how she got away with it. I've read the incident report, and the officers in charge put the incident down to a mere accident. Yet, you stated she threw things at him which hit his head. Maybe we can reopen the case and take a closer look at the postmortem report. Sorry, I'm just thinking out loud here. Did you continue to live in the house after the fire? Do you know if the insurance company paid out? I suppose they would if it was deemed an accident."

"Yes, they paid out on the *accident* claim. We moved house a few months later, once Mum got her claws into yet another man. He didn't last long, though, not once he started hitting her. Mum never allowed a man to dominate her in that way, ever. Actually, I'm surprised she didn't knife him. By the evil looks she gave him behind his back, I think the bloody thought often crossed her mind."

Lorne blew out a breath. "I guess he has to be considered a very lucky man. What about Claire's second husband?"

"She didn't marry again until around eight years later."

"Excuse me for butting in—how did your older sisters come about, then?"

"The odd fling that ended up in Mother unwisely falling pregnant. You'd think a woman who hates kids as much as she does would practice safe sex, wouldn't you? Not Mother! Anyway, she probably saw Deutschmark before her eyes when she married the next sucker."

"Are you telling me he was German?"

"Yes, he was Olga's dad, Heinrich Smitz."

"Ah, I see. My partner back in London passed on the general information about Claire's two marriages. However, she didn't go into any detail about the men. So what happened to Smitz?"

"The same thing. He appeared to burst into flames, according to the police report, this time during a barbecue, would you believe?"

"In front of you again?" Lorne asked, horrified.

"Yes, in front of *all* the kids. I was older then, around thirteen. I was the only one who really saw what actually happened, though. Heinrich was having fun. He was in charge of turning the food on the barbecue. Yes, he'd been drinking and was probably too far gone to think straight when the time came to fight for his life. He turned his back on the barbecue for a second to tell one of the girls off, I believe. Mum snuck up and tipped some alcohol on the barbecue. The bloody thing went up, and the flames leapt high into the sky. Poor Heinrich didn't stand a chance. The shock sent him off balance. When he turned to tackle the blaze, he stumbled on some cans lying at his feet and ended up face down on the grill. His clothes set alight, and he screamed. Mum shepherded the kids into the house. She was constantly looking over her shoulder. I tried my hardest to help him, but he was frantic, wouldn't let me near him. I tried to tackle him to the ground, knowing that if I rolled him, it would be possible to extinguish the flames, but he thrashed about. All that did was fan the flames. Suddenly, he collapsed to the ground. I pulled the tablecloth off the table, sent all the food and plates crashing. I didn't care. All I wanted to do was try and put out the flames. It was too late. When I reached him, his eyes were wide open. He was dead. My own father's fate ran through my mind at that instant. *She* did this. She killed both of them, but would the authorities listen to me? She denied everything. Every time I said anything, she swore blind I had an overexcited imagination and made me out to be a fool. It was not long after that I started running away from home. I lived in fear every night, too scared to sleep in case she snuck into my room to suffocate me. Yes, I had an overactive imagination in that respect—who wouldn't in the circumstances?"

"How dreadful. Sorry you had to witness such an awful incident. Okay, I'm going to request we open both files ASAP. She can't—and I won't allow her—to get away with this, Joe. You have my word on that. So you ran away from home. How many times?"

He contemplated her question for a few moments. "It must have been a dozen times or more. In those days, the police picked you up if they spotted you in the street, bundled you in the back of a panda car, slapped your wrist, and took you back home. I begged and pleaded for them to take me to a children's home, but they thought I was nuts. They told me that those places were the pits compared to the type of home I came from. Who gave them the right to think that? No one knew the living hell I went through at the hands of my mother. Every time they drove me home, she welcomed me with a loving hug and crocodile tears. Once the door was shut, she slapped my face, punched me a few times where the bruises wouldn't show, and locked me in my bedroom for days, without food and water. I found myself thinking the unthinkable, wishing that she would kill me. It would have been preferable to the existence I was being forced to lead. Eventually, I learned to do just that—exist. The day my sixteenth birthday arrived, I gave myself the best birthday present I could think of. I packed a suitcase and left—for good. My mother was pitiful, tried to block the door, but I gathered an almighty strength from somewhere deep within and tossed her aside in the hallway. Our relationship has been somewhat strained ever since."

"So you only turn up for weddings and funerals out of a sense of duty?"

"Yes. It pains me to say that. No man should feel such anger towards his family—or mother, to be more precise—like I do. However, people have to put themselves in my shoes before they start casting aspersions in my direction."

"You have no worries on that front concerning me, Joe. What else can you tell us about your mother or sisters that might help our investigation?"

Joe inhaled a deep breath. "From a very young age, Mother trained the girls to be like her. Showed them how to manipulate men, to achieve what they wanted and to not think twice about casting aside the men who refused to be compliant."

"What was her main objective? Money?"

He nodded. "Her one and only objective. Here's something you won't know: Mother is almost broke."

"What? How can that be? She divorced Allan but ended up with the house while he left the marital home empty-handed."

"Ah yes, this is where her greed faltered, though. She didn't realise that Allan was a secret gambler. He walked away with nothing. She thought he would give her a substantial sum to maintain the upkeep of the house. Wrong! The bills are crippling, especially living in the Fulham area. Still, I suppose it won't be long before she has yet another male victim in her bed, lavishing her with expensive gifts, loaning her thousands of pounds when she flutters her eyelashes, asking him to get her 'out of a financial blip'. That's usually how it works."

"I don't wish to appear rude, but do you really think that kind of strategy works on men, given your mother's age?"

He laughed briefly. "Have you seen how many desperate widowers there are sprinkled around London?"

"Don't they tend to go for much younger women?" Lorne asked, trying to fathom out the workings of a woman's mind who had spent her whole life spreading her legs to obtain access to their wallets.

"It depends. There's no doubting you get some men who prefer to be seen with a glamorous model-type hanging off their arm at functions. However there are also men who appear to be far more comfortable with an older, more experienced woman to keep them company in front of a glowing, open fire. It takes all sorts to make a world, as the saying goes."

"There's no doubting that motto in light of what I've learned about your family over the past week or so."

"Here's another thing likely to blow your mind, Lorne."

She tilted her head and asked, "What's that?"

"My mother employs a few staff—actually she's employed a lot over the years—who are or were illegal immigrants. She treats them like slaves, hands out less than minimum wage so they are forced to stay and work for her because they don't have the funds to move on. They live in the smallest room—depending on what house we're talking about, this could be the cellar or the attic—with bare essentials to their names. They're on call twenty-four hours a day for a pittance, which breaks my heart. Another situation that fuels the flames of hatred within me."

Lorne quickly scribbled down the notes as the cogs in her head began to churn. This valuable piece of information could get them a warrant for the house and eventually lead to an arrest. *Didn't a few of the notorious criminals in America get pulled over for the most innocuous of crimes such as driving offences or tax evasion?* "It's going to be hard to pin anything on your mother, as we've seen over the years, but this could be the lead we need to bring her down. Anything else?"

"I'm not sure how valid this information is, but I was walking down the stairs at the house when they were arranging things for the wake."

"At Lucy's house, right?"

"Yes, that's right. I overheard Mum and Teagan arguing about something. I strained my ear and heard a name crop up. I've never heard this name mentioned before, so have no idea what it relates to."

"Go on," Lorne asked, her pen ready for action.

"Barbara Stainforth. Forgive me if the name leads you up the wrong track. I'm just trying to give you all the information I can muster in the hope you can finally get my treacherous mother put away."

"Leave that with me. I can do a background check, see what we can come up with. Can you think of anything else, Joe? Not that you haven't given us a substantial amount of info already to be going on with."

"I think that's it. I hate to ask, knowing you have a lot to deal with right now, but could you possibly arrange the witness protection for me immediately? I have a feeling my mother will have a fair idea who has dished the dirt on her when you show up on her doorstep."

"Maybe she'll think that Olga has spilled the beans on all her wrongdoings over the years."

"Perhaps, although I doubt Olga will be able to remember much, what with the drugs addling her brain."

"She's told us enough. Now it's up to us to use what you've both given us to our advantage. Stay here. I'll check out the situation of a safe house and arrange for someone to take you there." Lorne reached across the table and patted the back of his hand. "I admire your courage in coming forward. Sorry for what this woman has subjected you to throughout your life, love."

"Thank you. Just promise me you'll do everything you can to end her vile reign over this family."

"You have my word on that, Joe."

Lorne left the room and returned to the interview room next door. She called Sally out into the hallway. "How's it going? Do we have enough to arrest Knight yet?"

"What's that twinkle in your eye, Lorne?"

She smiled and waved the notes she'd jotted down during the interview with Joe. "I think we have enough here to go after Claire Knight. I also think we should deal with this as a matter of urgency."

"I'm almost through here with Olga anyway. She's complaining she's tired. I'll send her back to her cell for a rest and dispose of Wallace's services then meet you back in the incident room. Can't wait to see what you have."

CHAPTER TWENTY

Lorne sat at her desk with two fresh cups of coffee sitting in front of her and waited patiently for Sally to arrive. Her friend stormed through the door and marched towards her wearing an anxious expression. She sat opposite Lorne and sipped at her coffee while Lorne ran through the major points in her notes.

"Wow, really? Slaves? That has to be the route we take to pull her in, doesn't it?"

Lorne raised a finger and tapped the side of her nose. "Let's try not to be too rash about arresting her on that count just yet. By all means, we can organise an arrest warrant on those charges, but Joe also came up with the name Barbara Stainforth." Lorne couldn't ignore the frown on Sally's face. "Okay, I'm thinking that name rings a bell with you."

Sally waved her hand uncertainly, twisting in her chair, and spoke to her partner. "Jack, do me a favour and conduct a search for Barbara Stainforth, will you?"

"The millionairess?"

"You know her?" Lorne asked Jack, her eyes bulging.

"Of course. Shame on you, Sally, for not recognising the name."

"Consider me bloody told off, then." Sally shook her head. "Nothing is springing to my mind, Jack. Let us have everything you can find out about her, pronto."

Jack tapped at his computer, and his printer churned to life moments later. Lorne and Sally studied the information he handed them.

"So, why do you think her name cropped up with the family?" Sally asked.

Lorne shook her head. "I have no idea. I think it would be worth paying Mrs. Stainforth a visit, though."

Sally rose from her chair, but Lorne caught her arm. "Wait a minute. I meant figuratively speaking, not us personally. I'm thinking we should send a male officer to see her, perhaps someone carrying a briefcase." Lorne winked at Sally.

"Why? What's the significance in that?" Sally asked.

"If we leave the family alone for a day or two, that could lead them to believe Olga hasn't told us much. If they've got plans on visiting this millionairess's home, it might spook them if you or I turn up. However, if they see a smartly dressed man call at the house carrying a briefcase, their interest will be piqued, but for a very different reason. Supposing we get Jack to go; if he turns up without a briefcase, then I'm thinking they'll presume he's a copper. If, on the other hand, he visits Mrs. Stainforth's house with a briefcase in hand, anyone watching might take that as a sign of Jack being from a financial background."

"Ahh… I'm with you now. What do you say, Jack? Are you up for it?"

"Of course. What do I do when I get there?"

"Once inside, out of earshot from any possible onlookers, I think you should ask Mrs. Stainforth if she has had any dealings with Claire Knight. Take it from there, Jack."

"All righty. My next question is, where do I get a bloody briefcase?"

Sally and Lorne shared an exasperated look. "Go to lost property, see if they have any lying around. I'd offer you mine, but it might be too girly for you," Sally replied.

Jack left the incident room and returned carrying a somewhat-battered black briefcase. He held it up in front of him. "Will this do?"

"That bloody thing is more battered than a piece of cod. It'll have to suffice. Let's run through things again before you leave. Ask the woman if she has any form of connection with Knight. Hopefully, you'll be able to gauge whether she needs our help rather than coming right out and asking her. If she does, then give her my direct number so that she can contact me. In the meantime, Lorne and I will put our heads together and see if we can formulate a plan to entice Knight and her entourage."

Jack was gone for about an hour before he came barging through the doors. "I hope you've conjured up a scheme, because we need to put that into action pretty damn quick."

"What's happened, Jack?" Sally asked.

"There's a meeting scheduled between the two ladies tomorrow."

"What?" Lorne sat upright in her chair. "Did you tell Mrs. Stainforth that you think she might be in trouble?"

Jack shook his head. "There was no need. She's aware of that already. She's scared shitless of Knight and her family but can't see a way out of the situation. I've told her we'll help all we can. She seemed relieved to hear that, said she'd been living on her nerves for months now. Everything escalated in the last week or so, since Ryan's death. They have something very bad over her."

"Bloody hell, man, get to the point!" Sally ordered.

He shrugged. "That's where she lost me, something about the deeds to the house."

Lorne chewed the inside of her mouth as she thought. "Didn't Olga mention something about taking papers from Daniel Grade, as well as robbing him of the cash?"

Sally nodded. "She did. Could that have been deeds? But Stainforth said that things had escalated since Ryan's death, not Grade's."

"You're right. What time is the meeting set up for, Jack?"

"Eleven in the morning," he replied, looking first at Sally and then Lorne in confusion.

"I think we should be there. Don't you, Sally?" Lorne smiled.

Sally nodded. "I wouldn't miss this for the world. I also think we should try and obtain the search warrants for all the family's properties and hit them at the same time. Can you organise the hits down in London, Lorne, with your partner?"

"Of course, I'll ring Katy now. Are you going to call Mrs. Stainforth to put her mind at rest and make her aware of what we're planning?"

"Let's get the warrants organised first, then I'd like you, me, and Jack to go over a plan of action for when we get to the house. I haven't quite sussed that part out just yet."

Lorne tapped the side of her nose. "I have an idea. I'll fill you in once I call London."

"I'll be all ears. Come on, Jack. Let's hit the phones, get a few backup teams organised."

Sally and Jack walked away with a spring in their steps, and Lorne had a good feeling tingling through her veins. She picked up her mobile and rang her partner. "Hey, Katy, I've got some good news. It's going to take a mammoth task to collaborate things, though. Have you got a pen and paper to hand?"

Her partner tutted and said sarcastically, "Hi, Katy. How are you feeling today? How's the baby? Still treating your stomach as a punch bag?"

"Oops, sorry, hon. Yes, all of the above. I'm so caught up with what's going on, my manners went to pot. How are you?" She tapped the pen impatiently on the desk.

Her partner laughed. "I was kidding. I know you of old. I don't have to be a bloody genius to know when you're excited, Lorne. Hit me with it. What do you need me to do?" After listening to the details of the plan they'd formulated, Katy gasped. "And you're expecting me to get warrants issued for tomorrow? You're not asking for much, are you?"

"Either you or Roberts. Go ask Sean to pull a few strings. We *need* this to happen tomorrow, Katy. It's vital we don't miss this opportunity to pull the rug from under this woman and her family." Lorne gave her partner a brief rundown of what Knight had been guilty of over the years. "Trust me when I say she's one cruel, heartless bitch who I'm going to take great pleasure in taking down."

Katy whistled. "Leave it with me. I'll get back to you when I've received the confirmation."

"Great news. Speak soon. Take care."

A few exhausting hours ticked by before the team had everything underway, then all they had to do was chew their fingernails and twiddle their thumbs until the permission came through for them to act upon the following day.

"All right, so once we get the warrants, how do we approach the house?" Sally asked Lorne as they scrutinised a plan of attack over a cup of coffee with Jack in Sally's office.

"My idea is to contact Mrs. Stainforth. Once we've worked things out, the last thing we want to do is scare her any more than she is already. If she's agreeable, I think you and I should get in the house early morning, perhaps around six, while it's still dark."

Sally nodded. "Sounds good. Then what?"

"We wait until Claire Knight arrives. I'm gambling on her showing up mob handed. Therefore, I think we should have undercover teams awaiting their arrival in the grounds."

"Are you intending to use the woman as bait?" Jack asked in a concerned voice.

"No. I thought we could ask Mrs. Stainforth to welcome the guests then make an excuse to leave the room," Lorne replied, unsure of that side of things just yet.

Sally shook her head. "She has staff, doesn't she, Jack?"

He nodded.

"Well, a member of staff could show Knight and her family through to the lounge. Lorne, you and I could be waiting for them in the room. As soon as they enter the house, we'll ensure the backup teams hit the house within moments of the family's arrival. Do we anticipate them having weapons?"

Lorne nodded thoughtfully. "I think we should. Are you Taser-trained, Sally?"

"No, not yet."

"Okay, I've just completed my basic training. I've not had the chance to use my skills as yet, but having a Taser with us will give us peace of mind—that and wearing vests, of course."

"You think they'll go all out on attack?"

"I'm not sure. It's better to be on our guard, just in case."

"Okay, let me ring Mrs. Stainforth and run through things with her, see if she offers any objections. Then I think we should call it a day, go home, and get some rest."

"Sounds good to me. I'll ring Tony, see how things are at home and bring him up to date on what's come to light." Lorne walked out of the office and sat at her temporary desk. "Hello, love. Is everything okay there?"

Tony let out a sigh, as if he'd been holding his breath for a while, waiting for her to ring. "Thought you'd forgotten us," he said, laughing.

"Never. It's been hectic. I tried to call several times, but you know how it is. Things crop up, needing your immediate attention. Anyway, I'm staying over another night."

"I figured that much. Is the case proving to be tougher than you first thought?"

"It never started out as being easy. We've pulled in one of the daughters and arrested her on a murder charge."

"Ryan's murder?"

"No. Katy called and said they had found DNA evidence placing the youngest daughter at the scene where that bank manager was killed. You remember the case that was reported last week? Until then, we didn't have any clues linking that crime to the family. Fortunately, we had DNA on file because of the girl's drug habit."

"Lucky you, not so lucky for her. So I'm guessing she's singing, breaking the family's trust in order to save her own skin. Am I right?"

"Kind of. She's told us a few interesting things, but the son has agreed to tell us a lot more in exchange for witness protection. Some of the stories he's told have sent shivers down my spine, hon. This is one cruel, with a capital C, bitch. Apparently, she treated the one and only boy in the family like shit, while she's set out to mould all four daughters into miniatures of herself."

"What about Ryan? Do you know who killed him?"

"Olga told us that two of her sisters killed him. We'll need to find evidence to back that up, though. Something else has grabbed our attention that we'll be acting upon in the morning."

"Go on. Don't keep me in suspense."

"We've organised search warrants for all the properties owned by the family in the hope that we'll find some kind of paper trail that will cause their demise. In the meantime, Sally and I are conducting a covert operation. We're going to trap the family as they attempt to coerce a millionairess into doing Lord knows what."

"That sounds like you're going in there to catch them in the act. Are you sure you want to go down that route, Lorne?"

"We haven't got any other option, love. We're seeing this as the only one open to us at this point. Our priority is to get this family tucked up behind bars before they kill anyone else. To my reckoning, Knight has four men's deaths on her hands, including two of her husbands from years ago. I have no idea how many more people have lost their lives in the interim period. For all we know, we could be looking at dozens. From what I can tell, when she focuses on something, she usually ends up getting it, no questions asked."

"Crap. Be careful. Devious people like that tend to have the ability to weigh up their options quickly and deal with any crisis that arises with astute accuracy. Be aware of that, and you'll be the one who emerges victorious."

Lorne laughed. "Are you teaching me how to suck eggs, Tony?"

"Not at all. All right, I'll shut up. I should have known better than to dish out advice to the formidable Lorne Warner."

"How's Charlie?"

"She's fine. Happy and upstairs getting ready for another date with Brandon."

"Wow, they seem to be keen on seeing a lot of each other."

"You worry too much. They're young and in love. Stop being jealous."

"You're nuts. I'm being a concerned mother; that's all," she said, cupping her hand around the phone so the rest of the team couldn't hear what she was saying.

"She's twenty-one, love. I'm sure she could teach you a thing or two about the birds and the bees, if you asked her."

"You reckon? Crap, I'm not up for that. I'll have a girly chat all the same when I get back. Right, I better go. We're still trying to formulate the plans so everything runs smoothly, from our end anyway. I'll let you know how it all pans out tomorrow."

"Good luck. I'll give Charlie your love. Miss you "

"I miss you too, sweetie." Lorne ended the call, sat back in her chair, and mulled over the conversation she would have with her daughter the minute she stepped back in the house. *God help me!*

CHAPTER TWENTY-ONE

The dreary weather the following morning matched Lorne's sombre mood. She and Sally picked out casual clothes to wear for the dangerous mission ahead of them. As a precaution, under their thick jumpers, they wore stab vests. Lorne's stomach was tied up in knots, leading her to refuse Sally's mother's kind offer of preparing a good breakfast for them. She would have struggled to keep the food down anyway. After a quick cup of coffee, Sally drove to Mrs. Stainforth's house. The woman had pre-arranged with one of her neighbours for Sally to park her car next door instead of leaving it in Stainforth's drive.

Keeping to the hedge-line of the garden, Lorne and Sally snuck around the back of the house, where Mrs. Stainforth's maid, Tilly, let them in. Mrs. Stainforth wafted down the stairs a few hours after their arrival. She chose not to speak with them until she'd had at least two cups of coffee, which infuriated Lorne.

Sally ran through the plans they had come up with to ensure that Mrs. Stainforth knew exactly what was expected of her. Then they waited, watching and listening to the ticking ornate grandfather clock in the living room until its hands reached 10:50 a.m.

Lorne clapped, drawing everyone's attention. "Okay, we need to get into position now. Tilly, you get ready to open the door."

The wafer-thin maid seemed petrified, and her clenched hands shook in front of her.

"You'll be safe. We're here, I promise. I want you to open the door with a big smile, all right? Can you show me that?"

Tilly smiled and constantly blinked as her mouth widened.

"That's it, perfect. No fear showing there." Lorne spoke to Mrs. Stainforth next. "You should go upstairs, lock yourself in your bedroom until we give you the all clear to come down. Please, don't be tempted to leave your room, no matter what you hear. Am I making myself clear?"

The woman nodded and inhaled a large breath.

"Don't worry. We have men surrounding the house. They're under strict instructions to storm the place as soon as Claire Knight, and whoever she has accompanying her, enters the property."

"It's all in hand, trust us," Sally added, giving the two petrified ladies the thumbs-up.

"I'll be glad when this is all over and I get my life back again," Mrs. Stainforth mumbled as she left the room.

Lorne placed a hand on Tilly's forearm. "Please, don't worry. Keep smiling, and nothing will happen to you, I swear."

"Yes, miss. I go to the door now and wait?"

"Just do what you would be doing normally, Tilly, until the bell rings."

The housekeeper scurried out of the room and turned towards the kitchen. Lorne inhaled and exhaled a few deep breaths. "Are you ready for this, Sally?"

Her friend's eyes widened, and she could see the uncertainty lying within.

Nevertheless, Sally nodded. "I'm ready. I'd be more anxious if I was alone, but having you by my side is very reassuring. Let's hope we can pull this off."

Lorne winked at Sally. Deep down, Lorne was feeling nervous, too. Working with Sally so far had been a breeze and had been enjoyable, but their working relationship hadn't really been put to the test. In Lorne's experience, women suspects could be far more dangerous than their male counterparts. Women could be vicious in their intent during an arrest, and from what they'd already learned about the family, Claire Knight's intent and impatience had been visible from the beginning of the investigation. Lorne cocked an ear in the air and raised a finger, signifying she'd heard the noise of a car door. "Right, here we go. Don't think about it; follow my lead. Most important of all, Sally, keep your distance and remain vigilant at all times, no matter what. Got that?"

Sally puffed out her cheeks and chewed on her lip. "I've got it." She clenched her fist and butted it against Lorne's in a sign of solidarity.

"We can do this. You stand by the mantelpiece and face the fire, and I'll sit in the nearby chair. Make sure they don't twig who we are until the front door is closed and they're all inside the house. That's all the indication the response team need to set their part of the plan in motion."

When the doorbell rang, Tilly's flip-flops slapped against the marbled tiles in the hallway. Lorne closed her eyes. *Pete, I know I haven't talked to you lately, but if you're around, please watch over us. Guide me if necessary.* She heard Tilly welcome Claire Knight and invite her into the lounge where Sally and Lorne were waiting.

"Miss, the lady and her family are here," Tilly addressed Lorne before she let out a squeal.

Lorne jumped out of her seat as Sally turned to face the family, all four of them. "Let her go. She's only doing her job."

Teagan raised the housekeeper's wrist and gave her a Chinese burn then pulled the woman against her, pressing her forearm against the woman's throat, restricting her airway. "If she wants to be part of this setup, then she has to learn to suffer the consequences of her actions."

"That's your forte, isn't it, Teagan? Causing innocent people physical pain? Is that what you enjoyed most when you killed Ryan?" Lorne goaded Teagan into admitting her role in her brother-in-law's death in front of Lucy. *Never let the criminals have the upper hand*, her father had instilled in her before she commenced her first day at the police training college.

Lucy's eyes bulged as she watched Teagan's face colour-up in guilt. Teagan's gaze narrowed and remained on Lorne. "She's trying to get a reaction out of us. Ignore her, Lucy."

Lorne smiled. "Is that so? I know you were one of the women seen boarding his boat the day of his death. What I haven't figured out yet is who your accomplice was."

Teagan's gaze momentarily darted in Helen's direction, and that told Lorne everything she needed to know. "Ah, I see. Helen, did Teagan kill Ryan? Or did you have the honour of carrying out the heinous crime?"

Helen blustered. Her terrified gaze volleyed between the other three members of her family. However, she remained silent, as if her tongue had swollen up in her mouth.

Lucy looked stunned. Claire, on the other hand, did not.

Lorne decided to go on the attack again and cause yet more anarchy. "That's not news to you though, is it, Claire?"

"Stop talking *shit*, Inspector."

"Am I really? Lucy, does your mother seem surprised by the news of Helen's involvement?"

Lucy shook her head, clearly mortified. "Now's the time to rid your soul of any underlying guilt you might be feeling, ladies. Feel free to fill in the gaps for your sister as to why you robbed her of her husband."

Teagan issued Helen a warning glance.

Lorne pounced again. "Helen, what if I put a lesser charge on the table for your involvement? How does that sound?"

Helen's head snapped round to face Lorne, and she blurted out, "I had nothing to do with it, I swear. It was all Teagan's fault. She killed him. I didn't know that it was her intention to kill him and set the boat alight. That was all news to me."

"Shut up! You fucking idiot!" Teagan's grip lessened on Tilly's throat. The woman tried to attempt an escape, but Teagan yanked her back and slapped her round the face. "Stay still, or I'll kill you next."

"No, you won't, Teagan. Your family have killed all the people you're going to kill. Given your penchant for disposing of husbands, I'm sure killing a mere housekeeper clearly wouldn't give you the same thrill."

Claire's eyes turned into narrowed slits. "Every one of them deserved to die. To challenge my instructions proved to be a very foolish act in the end... for all of them."

"So, Teagan killed Ryan under your instructions. Is that what you're saying, Claire?" Lorne pressed.

"No comment," Claire spat at Lorne.

"It's a little late to be bandying that around, Claire. Lucy, were you aware that your sisters were carrying out your mother's instructions?"

"No, totally unaware. Although everything is slotting into place now." Lucy stepped a few feet towards Lorne and turned to face her family. "Why? Why would you kill the one person in this world who gave me the security and love that I have craved for all these years?"

"Shut up, Lucy. She's fishing. We'll discuss this later. Let's just do what we've come here to do and get out of here."

Lorne reached around the back of her trousers and withdrew the Taser gun from her waistband. "I think we've foiled that plan, too, Claire. We have you covered. Teagan, let the woman go, or I'll hit your mother with thirty thousand volts."

The hesitation and the devilment that filled Teagan's eyes surprised Lorne.

It was her mother who pulled her up on her behaviour. "Teagan? Are you going to allow her to speak to you like that?"

"For once in your life, Mother, shut the fuck up and leave things to me." Suddenly, before Lorne could point the Taser in Teagan's direction, she pulled a knife from the back of her trousers and held it close to Tilly's throat. Lorne shook her head when she saw a trickle of blood seep from a nick in her flesh onto Tilly's white blouse. "Drop your weapon, Inspector, or I *will* kill her."

Out of the corner of her eye, Lorne saw Sally turn her way, apparently debating what to do next. The decision was swiftly taken out of her hands when the front door broke down. Tilly somehow managed to slip out of Teagan's grasp, and she ran towards Lorne, who pulled the trigger. Screams rang out from the family of women as Teagan dropped to the floor and thrashed around like a recently snared barracuda on the end of a fisherman's taut line.

"Stop it. You're going to kill her!" Claire shouted.

Lorne released the trigger. Two armed officers pounced on Teagan to ensure her injuries weren't fatal as officers from the tactical team rounded up the other family members.

Sally patted Lorne on the back. "Good job. I bet she regrets taking on the mighty Lorne Warner now."

"Not a bad shot, eh? I still feel bad for releasing the damn thing, but she pushed me into it. Are you all right, Tilly?" Lorne asked the housekeeper, peering at the slight wound to her neck.

"Yes, miss. Thank you." Tilly hugged Lorne and heaved a big sigh.

"Sergeant, can you ensure this young lady goes to hospital to get treatment for her wound?"

"Come with me, miss. We'll get you sorted," the officer said with a smile.

Lorne stepped towards Claire and stood inches in front of the woman, their gazes locked. "That's your little game ended, Knight. I can't wait to hear you try and talk your way out of this one."

"You haven't got a clue, bitch. You think you know everything about me, but you *don't*. My drugged-up daughter is aware of very little to do with my life."

"You're probably right. However, I have another ace up my sleeve that will help bring you down, actually several of them now you're in custody."

"Bollocks! No one dares to speak out against me."

"Oh, but they have, Knight. Do you really trust the other members of your family not to dish the dirt on the crimes you've apparently got away with over the years? Of course, we'll be offering them some kind of deal in exchange. That's kind of how you've run your life, isn't it? A deal here, another deal there, all involving men with huge bank accounts and bulging assets, right?"

Claire stared at Lorne but refused to reply.

"Go on, say it. 'No comment'. Take her away, boys. She might come across as being a lady, but don't hold back on showing her how we treat criminals, especially murderers. Here, let me have the honour of cuffing her." Lorne spun Claire around and slapped the cuffs intentionally against the woman's bony wrist.

"I'll get you for that, Warner."

"In your dreams maybe, Knight." Lorne shoved the woman towards the heavy-set officer, who led the way out of the house. Each of his men accompanied a cuffed member of the family.

"Back to the station?" Sally asked.

Lorne smiled. "I think we better rescue Mrs. Stainforth first, tell her that it's safe to come downstairs." She rushed up the stairs to fetch the woman. She knocked on the bedroom door. "Mrs. Stainforth, it's DI Warner, it's safe to come out now."

Mrs. Stainforth tentatively opened the door and descended the stairs. Halfway down, she tugged at Lorne's arm. "Are you sure it's safe to come down?"

"Of course. We're pretty confident we've got enough on Knight to lock her away for years this time."

"You don't know what a relief it is to hear you say that, Inspector. I really can't thank you enough."

"We'll need a statement from you, Mrs. Stainforth. Do you think you'll be able to sit down with Sally over the next few days and give us one?"

"Of course, I'll do anything and everything to help keep those women away from me."

Lorne and Sally left the residence, shook hands with the tactical team captain, and jumped in the car.

"To be honest, I had my doubts we'd be able to pull it off," Lorne said as Sally eased the car out of the neighbour's drive and drove back to the station.

"Really? You could have fooled me. You're so damn cool when adversity strikes."

Lorne shook her head and laughed. "Maybe you've got a point there, Sally. Lord knows I've had years of practice."

EPILOGUE

Once all the arrests and charges had been made on the family, Lorne returned to London, a feeling of satisfaction shrouding her like a comforting blanket.

Her own team erupted when she walked into the incident room. Lorne applauded them in return. "You guys are awesome. You did a fantastic job. Katy, do you want to join me in the office and bring me up to date on how the searches went?"

Katy nodded and followed Lorne into her office. "Wow, I really didn't think we would crack this case, Lorne."

"To be honest, neither did I. Bloody Knight has got away with murder for years. I'm still not sure how we managed to put her in the frame. Maybe she hasn't trained her kids well after all."

Katy reached for a file sitting on Lorne's desk and handed it to her. "This will make interesting reading."

Lorne glanced at her watch. It was almost six o'clock. "I think I'll take it home to read. As long as we've got enough to put them away for years, that's all that matters."

"Oh, we've got that all right. I'll give you a brief summary. We found evidence of fraud at each family member's homes. In some cases, the evidence wasn't even locked away."

"Let me guess, at either Helen's or Olga's house, right?"

"Spot on. Also, at Teagan's, we found the evidence that proves she was on that boat with Ryan."

"Interesting. What was that?" Lorne asked, sitting down behind her desk and letting out a weary sigh.

Katy sat opposite Lorne and linked her fingers across her tummy. "Some papers he'd drawn up. Deeds, in fact."

"Okay, simple question. How does that prove she was aboard the boat?"

"Because of the date. They were drawn up on the Friday before he was murdered."

Lorne chewed her lip. "Not exactly concrete evidence, but I can see there's a tenuous link for sure. Let's hope we can make it stick."

Katy nodded. "Even if that fails, we have her clothes with blood spatter that she tried to hide in a box in her wardrobe. I'm sure once the results come back from Forensics, it'll prove to be Ryan's."

"Plus, we have a statement from Olga telling us that both Teagan and Helen were involved in his murder. I think we'll be able to substantiate those claims now, just in case a judge threw it out of court due to the information coming from a questionable source."

"I understand that. We've also got the brother's statement, plus what happened at the Stainforth house, and over the next few days, I'm going to be trawling through the cold cases concerning Claire Knight. They won't get away with this, Lorne, none of them."

"Joe Knight mentioned that Lucy wasn't the angel she pretends to be, either. Still, I genuinely believe that she had nothing to do with her husband's death. Once the reality of Teagan and Helen murdering Ryan sets in, I'm sure she'll be singing to her heart's content. I don't suppose you've had the chance to ring Allan Watts yet and bring him up to date on what's occurred?"

"No, not yet. Are you thinking that with Knight now behind bars, he might consider throwing some shit her way, too?"

"Most definitely. I know I would if I were in his position and there was an opportunity of getting my beautiful home back."

"Point taken. Okay, I'm going to shoot off now, if that's okay with you?"

"Of course. Take care of the little one. Do you want to come in later in the morning?"

Katy tutted. "No special treatment, remember?"

"I know what we agreed, but we hadn't anticipated you taking charge again. You look drained, hon."

Katy stood up and moved towards the door. "Whatever. Go home to your family, Lorne."

Half an hour flew past before Lorne finally conceded that she was tired. She pulled herself away from the engrossing files and left the station. She arrived home to find Tony standing on the doorstep, wearing a huge grin, obviously pleased to see her. "I've missed you so much." She kissed him and held him tightly.

"So glad you and Sally finally caught the buggers. Are you ready for some dinner? I have a bit of a surprise inside for you."

"You mean you've prepared a char-free dinner for a change?" she ribbed him.

"There are plenty of women out there who would snap me up with a click of the fingers, Lorne Warner. You seem to forget that occasionally. Maybe I should start trawling through that little black book I have tucked away in the back of my wardrobe for one of my many admirers from my agent days."

Lorne thumped his arm. "You dare, mister!"

He gripped her hand and led her into the kitchen. She gasped when she saw the mountain of stuff lying on the kitchen table. "Ta, da!"

Lorne frowned and stepped closer. The items consisted mostly of children's clothes and games. "Have you been to a jumble sale? What is all this, Tony?"

"I thought I'd help out for a change and buy Jade's kids their Christmas presents."

"Really? This is *all* for them?"

He looked worried. "Damn, have I gone over the top?"

Lorne laughed. "To me, yes, but to Jade, I doubt you've gone far enough." She shook her head. "What did I do to deserve a thoughtful, considerate man like you?"

Tony shrugged. "Lucky, I guess. Now, let's forget dinner and go upstairs, then you can show me how grateful you are that I'm such a thoughtful, considerate husband."

The End

Made in the USA
San Bernardino, CA
06 October 2017